Master Gunslingers Revenge

by
Steven R. Smyrski

Order this book online at www.trafford.com
or email orders@trafford.com

Most Trafford titles are also available at major online book retailers.

This is a work of fiction. All of the characters, names, incidents,
organizations, and dialogue in this novel are either the products
of the author's imagination or are used fictitiously.

Printed in the United States of America.

ISBN: 978-1-4269-4532-8 (sc)
ISBN: 978-1-4269-4533-5 (e)

Trafford rev. 11/21/2010

 www.trafford.com

North America & international
toll-free: 1 888 232 4444 (USA & Canada)
phone: 250 383 6864 ♦ fax: 812 355 4082

Vince Masters

The

MASTER GUNSLINGERS
REVENGE

By Steven R. Smyrski

Introduction

"You boys need something?" Vince asked inquisitively.

"Well since you had the nerve to walk over and disturb our conversation," one of the men answered. "We saw you come in with that other fella. You have something to do with him? The rest of his folks high tailed it out of town weeks ago. You helping him pack to leave too?" Laughing to his buddy.

"Can't see where that would be any of your business, but to answer your question the answer is no. I'm gonna be working with him in breeding cattle," Vince replied with authority. "By the way we're looking for cattle rustlers that are helping themselves to local stock and we aim to find out who. Either of you know anything about that?"

"I don't know if we like the way you're talking to us friend," one growled back.

"Are you accusing us of taking your cattle?"

"If you have nothing to hide then it shouldn't bother you, and I'm not your friend," Vince answered roughly.

The bigger of the two men stood up.

"I ought to pistol whip you right here," he threatened.

Before he had it all out of his mouth there was a pistol barrel being pushed real hard in his ribs.

"Well maybe I ought to shoot you right here," Vince retaliated. "Now sit down and shut up. If you know who's behind the rustling let them know it had better cease. Savvy?"

Moments latter the two men retreated toward the batwings.

"You aint heard the last of this, I promise you that," one said as he retreated.

CHAPTER 1

The streets were sloppy, muddy with ruts six inches deep. New buds were growing on once bare limbs of trees hinting that winter was over, announcing that spring was here. Heavy coats being replaced by sweaters or vests over shirts. Birds were singing making nests to start reproduction. Dogs were shedding hair as they ran. Some scratching annoying fleas out doors on the side walks. Still, it was a dark and gloomy day. The sun had been battling heavy cloud cover for days yet able to keep the temperature to a comfortable level.

People who normally stayed inside for warm were now outdoors enjoying the warm spring air. The General Store selling supplies as fast as they were delivered. This was Saturday. Kids were running and getting in everyone's way as their mothers were doing the shopping.

This past year was one Vince would like to forget, for the most part, yet a lot happened that he would always treasure. He killed four men who forced his draw. His quickness allowed him to survive. He accomplished his mission to find the killer of his family, yet able to keep his identity as a gunfighter unknown. It was now time for him and his wife Jane to find a place to settle and raise a family. She was eight months pregnant and the trip had taken its toll on her.

If only Vince knew what was waiting for him in Colorado. He hoped to settle and raise cattle. Danger was in his future however and his ability to handle a gun would again save him.

On this particular morning Vince and Jane slept-in having no plans of importance for the day.

"Breakfast anyone?" He teased. "I'm so hungry I could eat a horse."

"You go eat a horse and I'll stay here in bed," she replied.

"Come on, get up. I don't want to eat by myself. The day's awastin," Vince answered back.

"Ok, ok, but you're going to have to wait. I look just awful," she moaned.

About forty five minutes later they were on their way down to brunch. Vince was chomping at the bit. "Women," he mumbled to himself.

The place already looked deserted. It was almost lunch time. There was no trouble finding a table or getting served quickly. Vince looked around by habit, checking the surroundings.

Today was the day he hoped to meet up with his friend Jeb. He would ask around where Jeb's brother's ranch was located. It had been a long journey and both were glad it was nearly over.

Vince was not sure whether he should settle here in Colorado or head back to run his dad's ranch in Arkansas. Whatever the decision, it couldn't happen until his child was born and old enough to travel. Alamosa would be a town to make do for now with plenty of time to decide if this might be a place to raise a family. Vince thought of how much nicer the country was the further west they rode.

Finishing their meal, Vince paid the server and they left. The sun was finally breaking through the clouds warming everything. This didn't bother Vince but Jane was carrying extra baggage, so it did her.

Walking down the walk Vince heard a voice.

"Hold it right there mister, you're under arrest so please don't resist," came the voice from behind.

Vince turned knowing who gave the warning and was more than happy to respond.

Jeb gave Vince a hug and a slap on the back. Looking Jane up and down observing her pillow-stuffed looking tummy he gave her a tender, careful hug, kissing her on the cheek.

"You two are a sight for sore eyes. I figured you two had gone back east to your dad's ranch. When did you get in?" He asked anxiously.

"Late yesterday afternoon," Vince answered.

"Come, I'll buy you lunch," Jeb offered.

"Thanks Jeb but we just finished breakfast," he confessed.

"I hope you'll be staying. My place is only six miles south. You'll stay with me, won't you?" He asked.

"Sure. Let me get the wagon and we'll follow you," Vince responded.

Pulling up to Jebs place Vince could feel Colt and Starlight pulling at the lead rope, acting antsy, hoping they weren't going to be dragged across country any farther.

The cabin looked new and quite homey. Just in-sight up on a mound was the bunk house of the ranch hands. A weak light was showing softly through each of the front windows.

Jeb rushed over helping with the baggage carrying it to the porch. It was quite nice and as they walked-in Jane could see right off this was a man's cabin. She immediately thought it could use a woman's touch. She was already brain storming the changes she would make while visiting.

Jeb was reading her mind as he watched her observe the living area, but would tolerate any changes. Having company would be nice as Vince and Jane were his first visitors since the place was finished.

"How long can you stay?" He asked bringing the baggage inside the doorway while nodding to the second bedroom where they would bed down.

"Not sure yet. With Jane's condition and all it may be awhile. Thought we'd look around and see if maybe this would be a place to settle. If not, we'd head back to Arkansas," he answered.

"Well, you're more than welcome to stay as long as you please. I really mean it," Jeb gestured. "Sit. Make yourself at home. You must be tired, how was your trip?" looking to Jane for the answer.

"Long. Real, real long," Jane answered, holding her hands under her tummy.

For the next hour the three sat and caught up on things, talking of old times but leaving out the killing or the arrest of the killer Vince had finally caught up to. That could be talked about between the two men at a later time.

"Jane can unpack while you and I bring in the clothes cases. I'll unhitch the wagons and get the horses settled," Jeb offered.

Once out in the barn Vince could see concern in Jeb's eyes. They had traveled miles together in the years past so Vince picked up on it at once.

"Ok, out with it," Vince ordered. "I can tell when something's on your mind so what is it?

"Heck, Vince you just got here, I don't need to lay my troubles on you. You just got over your own devastation not too long ago, which by the way you'll need to fill me in on how that all went down. The paper here isn't the most reliable and the story told was very sketchy and I'm sure exaggerated," Jeb noted.

"Alright I won't press you tonight, you can tell me everything tomorrow, right?" Vince commanded.

"There will plenty of time to talk," Jeb promised.

The rest of the time was spent on small talk as they brushed down and fed the horses. All four horses looked like they could put weight on. Even Colt and Silver Star looked as if they lost some of their shine.

By the time they got back to the house Jane had nosed around and found enough grub to fix a small dinner which was quickly devoured.

CHAPTER 2

The next morning after a good breakfast Jeb disappeared to the bunk house. He saddled the horses and returned to fetch Vince to ride out to see his herd. Colt was ready. The morning weather so cool Vince gave him the rein and let him go. In a few minutes of bucking and running he settled after getting Vince's pull at the reins. Vince had Jeb ride Black Star knowing he had to be ridden.

It took a half hour to get to the hill where both men would sit looking down on at least fifteen hundred head. Vince was immediately impressed. Fine looking cattle all close together grazing some of the greenest grass Vince had ever seen.

"Man, what a fine looking herd friend," Vince complimented.

"Yeah, but holding on to them is another thing. Vince, you asked me last night why I look so bothersome. Well it's just that each month I'm missing fifty to seventy head. I have no idea who or how. It's not only my cattle but my neighbors also. I could use your help," he pleaded.

"You know you can count on me to help anyway I can, what about your brothers?" Vince asked.

"They sold out to me. They had the same trouble but also they're families were threatened every time they went to town. They thought it safer for the family to sell out and move to California. I bought them out after I couldn't talk them into letting me help them get to the bottom of it, but then again I'm single. They made the right choice because this has me baffled and I think it's going to get dangerous the longer it goes on. The cattle are branded but none are showing up anywhere. It's like they're just disappearing into the thin air," Jeb commented.

Vince sat there looking off in the distance rubbing his chin deep in thought. Maybe later he would ride out and look around his self for clues. If Jeb was asking for help then he must be real desperate. Vince knew how Jeb stood by him while he searched for the man who killed his family so he definitely would help his friend find and put his problem to rest.

While he was looking over the herd he thought he saw something way out in the distance. He cleared his eyes and looked closely again looking for movement but saw nothing. What ever he thought he saw was gone or really wasn't there. His mind was burning in thought of how he could help his friend.

Who were these men threatening Jeb's brothers and their families? Could they want their land, instigate trouble to intimidate the family's for them to sell? It had to be real bad to make families leave their homes and land to insure safety. Thinking of what action he would take he decided to take a trip to town and look around. He would do that later with Jeb and let anyone in town who was interested see that Jeb was not riding solo any longer. That he had a concerned friend who would welcome anyone to lay their cards on the table to what they really wanted. All of a sudden his thoughts were interrupted when Jeb rode up.

"Let's head back, I want to show you the rest of the ranch," Jeb announced.

"Who are these men who are giving you trouble?" Vince asked.

"I can't put my finger on just one. Who ever is doing this is using their brains. I believe they are working in groups and answering to one man. If I'm right the leader is very rich and buying men who are faithful or intimidated enough to keep their mouth shut. Even the Sheriff has little information to go on and won't act until he has real proof. I can't blame him for he'd sure look foolish if he accused the wrong men," Jeb admitted.

"I'd like to ride into town with you later letting whoever's involved see that you're not by yourself any longer. Maybe we can ruffle some feathers and force someone to make a mistake. What do you think?" Vince asked.

"Sounds like it could get pretty interesting," Jeb admitted.

Jeb was relieved to have Vince on the ranch with him. He knew he couldn't do much on his own and Sheriff Parker wasn't being much of a help. One thing he didn't want was to put Vince in any danger. He was married and going to be a father. Getting him involved made him uneasy even if it was Vince's idea.

"Do you know any of the trouble makers or have any thoughts of who the kingpin could be?" Vince asked. "Is there anyone trying to buy you out or force you out?"

"No to either. My brothers couldn't describe any one man. It seemed when anything was said it was through a third person or a group of men who would alibi for each other if questioned or if trouble was pursued." Jeb answered.

The weather was cooperating in every way. Not a cloud in the sky keeping the temperature stable and consistently comfortable. If the weather would stay this way till Jane had the baby Vince knew she'd really appreciate it. It was perfect riding weather. To ride a ranch this size it would take days maybe even a week. He knew he could depend on Colt as he was being playful enjoying the weather too.

Jeb rode with Vince bringing him to the top of a hill where you could see for miles.

"Beautiful huh buddy?" Jeb asked.

Vince sat on Colt and gave a Panasonic swipe looking at miles of the most beautiful land anyone could imagine. He was looking at mountain ranges that lasted as far as the eye could see. Some of the greenest land he had ever seen. Down at the bottom was the bluest lakes fed by the clearest brooks. He was facing west imagining how nice the sunsets probably were. He told himself he would bring Jane up one evening to watch the sunset.

"I know. You're gonna ask me why I didn't build here. Right?" Jeb asked. "Almost everyone I've brought here asks the same thing. My answer is always the same. Had I rode up here before I built the house this would have been the exact spot to where I would have."

"I can't believe your brothers would pick up stakes and leave this land for any reason. This is definitely worth fighting for," Vince surrendered.

"I feel the same way, but I also know they had to do what it took to keep their families safe." Jeb answered sincerely.

"We'll get to the bottom of this and straighten everything out. I promise you right here and now, I'm in this for the duration," Vince answered.

"You're a good friend Vince. I knew you were a good man the day I met you," Jeb complimented.

They spent most late afternoon admiring the rest of the ranch on horseback. Most of which was the most beautiful land Vince had ever put sight on. The cattle Jeb was raising was some of the best bred money could buy. Vince couldn't help thinking of his father and how much time and work it took to have cattle of such quality. This made him very sad.

Later that afternoon Vince and Jeb rode to town. Vince knew if there was a chance of learning anything about missing cattle, it would be there. Or at least he hoped.

Riding into town they reminisced over the journey and the adventures they shared the past year. They both agreed they were lucky to still be alive. To Vince it was like starting all over again. He knew he would have to be very careful as he was a husband now and to be a father soon. He knew how important it would be to survive to watch his little one grow.

As they rode into town Vince stayed alert as he knew Jeb was. They pulled up to the front of the saloon and tied the horses.

"I could sure use a beer," were the first words out of Jebs mouth.

"I hear that," Vince responded.

It was still early; they had the saloon almost to themselves. It was no trouble finding a place at the bar.

"How about a couple of beers over here Ben for me and my friend," Jeb asked.

"Coming up," was answered.

"This here is my friend Vince," he introduced to Ben. "Vince, this here's Ben, the owner of this fine establishment."

Vince looked around noticing this was quite a nice place. Not the place riff raff would hang around. Ben was a pretty big fella looking capable of escorting almost any size trouble maker right out those batwings into the street.

"Your stayin here in Alamoa, Vince?" Ben asked.

"Nothing decided Ben, just visiting for now. Came out to see my friend Jeb here and check out the lay of the land. My wife is going to have our first child any time so we'll be staying with Jeb. I have a ranch back in Arkansas so I will have a decision to make in a few months," Vince answered.

"Sounds like you do Vince," Ben agreed. "Doc Sanders is one of the best. Met him yet?" Ben asked.

"No, but it probably wouldn't hurt to stop and meet him before I leave," Vince responded. "I'm sure he'll want to see my wife pretty soon."

Vince noticed two men sitting at a table off to the right. It seemed to him he was being studied by both. They were far enough away he didn't think they could hear any of their conversation but something told him they were trying.

"Those two over to the left, seen them before?" He asked Jeb in a low voice.

Nonchalantly Jeb gave a slow glance so he could see them out of the corner of his eye.

"Nope, can't say that I have," he responded.

"Well they sure have been checking us out pretty good. Think I'll go see what's on their mind," Vince announced.

He turned heel and walked over to the table. This took both men by surprise as they weren't expecting this.

Both men stopped their conversation since it was about Jeb, Vince, or both.

"You boys need something?" Vince asked inquisitively.

"Well since you had the nerve to walk over and disturb our conversation," one of the men answered. "We saw you come in with that other fella. You have something to do with him? The rest of his folks high tailed it out of town weeks ago. You helping him pack and leave too?" Laughing to his buddy.

"Can't see where that would be any of your business, but to answer your question the answer is no. I'm gonna be working with him in breeding cattle," Vince replied with authority. "By the way we're looking for cattle rustlers that are helping themselves to local stock and we aim to find out who, either of you know anything about that?"

"I don't know if we like the way you're talking to us friend," one growled back. "Are you accusing us of taking your cattle?

"If you have nothing to hide then it shouldn't bother you, and I'm not your friend," Vince answered roughly.

The bigger of the two men stood up.

"I ought to pistol whip you right here," he threatened.

Before he had it all out of his mouth there was a pistol barrel being pushed real hard in his ribs.

"Well, maybe I ought to shoot you right here," Vince retaliated. "Now sit down and shut up. If you know who's behind the rustling let them know it had better cease. Savvy?"

Moments later both men retreated toward the batwings.

"You ain't heard the last of this, I promise you that," one said as he retreated.

As Vince walked back to Jeb he could see he was about to say something.

"What?" Vince asked without waiting.

"Don't know if that was a very good move," Jeb asked.

"What better way of getting it out that we mean business," he answered.

"I'm sure if those two are involved they're small potatoes. We need to find the master mind. How they're doing this is pretty mystifying," Vince conceded.

"When was the last time you discovered missing cattle?" Vince asked.

"Been a while so it may be time to keep an eye on things," Jeb responded.

Finishing his beer Vince let his mind wander to how cattle could be disappearing without any trace. Then he switched his thoughts to what he had done. He knew he should have handled that big fella a different way. Why didn't he just grab him by his collar and jack his ass up. Why did he show his cards and pull his gun. Stupid move for a guy trying to hide his gunmanship he thought.

CHAPTER 3

Jack and Frank rode up to the front of the hidden cabin down in the valley. Waiting for them was the spokesman for the gang leader who insisted on staying unknown.

"Well what did you find out?" He asked the two.

"We found out that Jed has a man staying at his ranch helping investigate the missing cattle," Frank answered.

"He the law?" the man asked.

"I don't think so; I think he's a hired gun. He got into a confrontation with Jack and when Jack threatened him he pulled a gun without us ever seeing it," Frank admitted.

"Then he ain't a hired gun or else Jack would be dead. But that doesn't mean he ain't the law," the man responded. "We better leave his spread alone for a while. Maybe we can throw them off. Next time you two go to town lay low."

"Charlie Smith just brought in about eight hundred head, we'll go round up his strays. Johnson's ranch just had quite a herd brought in too," Frank reported.

"Ok, that should keep you busy for a while but be careful; this man could be investigating for all the ranchers. What about the sheriff? What's he up to?" the man asked.

"He came into the saloon but just making his rounds. He's investigated the missing cattle from the start and has no idea of what's going on. All the more reason I think Jeb's up to something," Frank reported.

"What's this guy's name?" The man asked.

"I don't remember hearing a name, they were too far away, we only caught bits and pieces but it was enough for this guy to catch us trying to ease drop," Frank confessed.

"Alright go on I'll see what I can find out, like I said you two hang low," the man warned.

Jack and Frank turned heel and left the cabin.

"What we gonna do now Frank?" Jack asked.

"You heard the man, we hang low," Frank responded.

It was starting to rain as they mounted. It was a ways back to Jacks place. Knowing they were in for a wet ride Frank adjusted his coat pulling the collar up and buttoning the top. Thinking of what was next for himself and Jack. He was very mad at himself for being so sloppy back in town. Who was this stranger hanging out with Jeb?

He thought back not remembering seeing the stranger pull his gun on Jack.

Chapter 4

Vince walked down to meet the Doctor. As he entered his office he was met by an elderly man with white hair and glasses. Vince introduced himself and explained the reason for the visit, telling him of Jane's condition and of the trip they had just completed. This concerned the Doc. His name was Adams, John Adams, but every one called him Doc or Doc Adams. He was a jolly sort and assured Vince everything should be fine. He said he would be out to examine Jane sometime tomorrow. A long trip like that could take a toll on a pregnant woman so far into pregnancy but if she was in good health and strong she should probably be fine. That was good news for Vince. He knew he would have to stay close to the ranch and wait with Jane for the doctor's arrival. After the doc's recommendations he would then decide how far from the ranch he could investigate. He knew somewhere there had to be clues and signs of where the missing cattle were taken. There could be no magic trick to this, there would have to be signs and he and Jeb would find them together.

Stepping outside as he left the office it began to rain. This was bad. He knew any clues now would be washed away. Looking up to the skies he saw that the rain was going to be around awhile. Staying at the ranch tomorrow with Jane to wait for the doctor made him feel good and knew Jane would appreciate it also. He would wait and in the next few days ride out and count cattle with Jeb. If cattle came up missing after the rain stopped there were sure to be some clues left in the moist turf.

The next morning while eating breakfast he asked Jeb if he could show him a map or draw the perimeter of the ranch on paper. The boundaries would be very important to Vince. It would be something to carry on his person at all times. Knowing Jeb wouldn't be with him all the time. He didn't want to be caught roaming on someone else's property.

He wanted to study all the mountains and valleys where it might be easy for cattle to be driven without being noticed.

It took Jeb a while to draw the map but when he finished and handed it to Vince; he could clearly see it was quite detailed in every way. He sat there and studied it for a while then folded it and slipped it into his coat pocket where he knew it would be when he wanted it.

Finishing breakfast the two men got up and cleaned off the table. They poured themselves cups of coffee and sat back down having small talk amongst themselves with Jane. She was glad the men decided to stay with her and wait for the doctor. She felt good but was anxious to hear it from the doctor that everything was fine. Vince had decided to spend the morning in the barn and tend to the horses. Colt had recently been ridden but Black Star was stabled too long and needed to be cleaned and ridden. He hoped the doctor would be by before noon so he could go wander around some and get acquainted with the rest of the ranch.

There was a knock at the door. Vince took it for granted that it was Doc Adams, but as he opened the door he was face to face with a stranger he hadn't seen before.

"Good morning," the stranger addressed. "I'm looking for Jeb."

"Good morning Charlie," Jeb greeted as he walked up behind Vince. "I'd like you to meet Vince a good friend of mine. Vince this is Charlie Smith. He owns the T-Bar ranch just over those hills," pointing in the direction of where his ranch was located.

"Won't you come in for coffee?"

"Sounds good to me," was the response as he walk on in.

Sitting down at the table Jeb introduced Jane to Charlie.

Pouring coffee for Charlie and refilling the other cups he asked, "So what brings you out here so early? Did you eat breakfast? We have plenty."

"No thanks, we ate already. What brings me out here is my concern over missing cattle. I bought three hundred head earlier this week. The hands are bringing them in sometime today. Ben Johnson has about the same. But we have the same problem as you. Every time we bring cattle in they seem to mysteriously thin out over time. I can't afford to let this keep happening as I'm sure you and Ben can't," Charlie confessed. "That's what brings me out. We have to come together as neighbors and stop this or we'll all be selling out as your brothers did."

"I don't think we need to get that drastic yet Charlie, but you're right and that's why Vince is here. He is going to help us figure this thing out," Jeb announced.

Just then there was another knock at the door.

"Come one in," Jeb yelled.

This time it was Doc Adams. He walked on in carrying his familiar black bag. Walked over to the table, took a big whiff, and said, "My, that coffee smells good."

Jeb poured a cup full for Doc and introduced everyone.

"Well you must be Jane. You look like you could spring any time, as he looked over her big belly which showed even through the loose dress she was wearing. We'll just have a look at ya in a bit," he said in his jolly way.

"I better get going," Charlie said as he stood up and brought his empty cup to the sink. "I hope we can get together real soon Jeb. I'm on my way over to see Ben and hope we can plan a time to discuss this further. Good day everyone. "

"The sooner the better, let's see what Doc has to say about Jane and then we can set a definite time," Jeb answered, walking Charlie to the door. Minutes later they heard the foot pounding of the doc's horse pulling him away in his little black buggy.

CHAPTER 5

Russell Hillman wanted to make a name for him self.

Traveling from town to town, state to state solo, this gun crazed killer robbed banks, trains, and stores. He found no problem in challenging a draw down for no real reason other than to build his ego. When surrounding towns learned he was in the territory it was known that it was only a matter of time before their town would become the Devil's playground.

It was a hot day in June. The sun was beating down showing no mercy to anyone or anything on earth's surface. It was afternoon and the sun was at its hottest.

There came the sound of a lone horse making its way down Main Street. The stranger was riding nonchalantly in the saddle holding the reins and the saddle horn with both hands. His hat was pulled down shielding his eyes from the bright sun.

His narrow eyes staring straight ahead as he rode, wanting no attention. He would mind his own business and wanted anyone around to do the same.

It had been a long hot ride. Not all easy as the way he had left the last town.

Three days ago he had been riding for his life, hard and fast with a pose of five hot on his heels. While robbing a gold office his actions were discovered almost getting him shot out of his saddle exiting town.

He had enough gold nuggets and dust to enable him to lay low for a while. When his stash started to run out he would rob again in another town. If it meant killing it would mean nothing to him. The stranger rode up to the front of the saloon on Main, climbed down from the saddle and reined his horse to the post bar. Standing on the walk he carefully rolled a cigarette, placed it in his mouth and struck a match on a porch post he was standing next to and lit it. Taking a panoramic look around the area checking for danger he took a long drag on the cigarette. Seeing none he turned heel and walked through the bat wings headed for the bar.

"How bout a beer and a shot of whiskey bar keep," he ordered.

The bartend filled the order right away then went back to wiping the bar top while waiting for patrons.

"Just getting to town stranger?" The bartender asked.

"Yeah," Russell answered. "It's so damned hot and dusty. Where can I get a bath?"

"If you're getting a room at the Queens Hotel they will be happy to accommodate you," answered the bartender.

"Thanks, I guess I will then," Russell retorted. "Does it get busy in the evening? Gamblers I mean. I'd like to get into a card game."

"Things should start hopping within the next few hours. Most of the cow pokes try to finish early on Fridays. Can't wait to loose their week's wages," the bartender answered. "Good looking guy like yourself ought to find a good looking lady when you're tired of cards."

Russell had a few more drinks while making small talk with the bartender and then excused himself to get his horse to the livery. After he walked to get a room and bath before the evening got started.

While walking out he was almost run over by a couple of men, Barry Slocomb and his buddy Brett Barnett. The two men who were ranch hands employed by Ben Johnson stormed through the bat wings using no caution that someone may be leaving. Neither excused themselves or paid any attention that they almost knocked over Russell while coming through heading for the bar. Russell usually would have made a deal of this but was too tired and wanted to care for his horse and get a bath so he brushed it off continuing on his way.

CHAPTER 6

Jane was walking from the bedroom to get a glass of water when she felt a sharp pain. Being only eight months pregnant she didn't think too much of it. She poured her water and went so sit at the table when she received another pain, this time sharper than the last.

"Vince honey, get in here," Jane yelled.

Vince and Jeb both came in to see what she needed.

"What is it sweetheart?" Vince asked.

Cupping her belly with hands she looked up with a scared look on her face.

"Go get Doc Adams," she responded. "He couldn't be too far. Oh Damn!"

Looking down to see she was now sitting in water.

"Now Vince. Please go," she hollered.

Vince was out the door in a flash. Colt seemed ready as he slipped the reins over his head. Not taking the time to saddle Colt he was riding out of the barn bare back holding his legs tight to Colts body as he went through his bucking ritual. Catching up to the Doc's wagon within minutes,

Vince was yelling to stop him, but not until Vince was up next to the wagon did Doc hear him.

Pulling back on the reins he already knew why Vince was stopping him.

Four hours later patiently waiting, Vince finally heard the cry. He was now a dad.

He rushed in to check on Jane when he met the Doc coming out of the bedroom wiping his hands smiling when he saw Vince.

"It's a boy," he announced holding out his hand to shake. "They're both fine. You can go in and see them but your wife is very tired so make it short, she'll need a lot of rest."

He entered the room and Jane was lying there with the baby on her tummy.

"Come honey, come see our son, Richard," she invited in a soft tired voice.

Vince, as tough as he was, shared tears with her knowing the baby was named after his father. He reached and fluffed the pillow to make her more comfortable, then took a long hard look at his son. With a smile he kissed them both promising he would be right outside if she needed anything, pulling the cover up to comfort them, he turned and left the room shutting the door behind him.

"Thanks Doc, for everything," handing him a lump sum of bills knowing it was more than his fee would have been. "You come back and check on them soon."

"I'll be back tomorrow sometime," he promised as he put on his hat and left.

"A boy Jeb, how lucky can a man be," he bragged.

"Let's go sit out on the porch, we'll be able to hear if she needs us," he assured Vince.

CHAPTER 7

Barry Slocomb and Brett Barnett were hugging up to the bar finishing a beer when they notice a card game going on with two empty seats.

"Shall we," Barry asked Brett. "I feel lucky."

"If I had a nickel for every time I've heard that I wouldn't have to gamble. I'd be too busy counting nickels," Brett teased as they headed for the table.

In just a few hands Barry had scooped up a fare amount of winnings.

"I guess you were feeling lucky," Brett commented.

One of the men at the table stood up and excused himself announcing he had lost enough for one night. As he left the chair it became occupied immediately by another man. No one knew but the man who just sat down was Russell Hillman.

"What's the stakes here?" He asked.

"This here's a friendly game mister," a man who everyone was calling Buster answered. "No bodies complained about a limit so far so if you think you have the cards, bet. Anyone who can't keep up can fold."

Another player at the table was Matt. He didn't say much, just played his own game by watching for weaknesses in the others. He had quite a stack of winning in front of him showing he wasn't new to the game.

Russell right away took special interest in Matt. He didn't say anything as he watched the other players trying to catch any signs of bluffing. He had Barry figured out already the way one side of his upper lip would curve up while adjusting his cards. Brett didn't need too much attention as he played foolish and bet carelessly just to stay in. He wasn't loosing too badly but on the flip side he wasn't raking in much either. Buster was as he said, playing a friendly game. When stakes got too high, unless he knew for sure he had a winning hand he would throw in early. Russell thought he was playing to stay out of the house. Probably had a nag for a wife or a house full of kids or worse, both. His attention went back to Matt.

"You from around these parts?" Russsell asked Matt.

"Nope just here for a few days and then moving on," Matt answered.

"How about you?" Matt returned the question.

"Just got to town today, thinking of staying a while, see if I can pick up a job with one of the local ranchers," he lied back to Matt.

"Charlie Smith is looking for a couple of good men to run cattle," Brett offered. "He has one of the bigger cattle ranches around. His ranch is about three miles west out of town."

"Thanks," Russell answered not having any intentions of getting a job.

Russell wasn't looking for trouble so soon but his eye caught something Matt did with the cards. He played a few hands trying to figure out what was being pulled. The others had been drinking so their eyes would be missing any cheating but not being much of a drinker Russell was still alert to see that Matt knowing their condition was doping money from the others.

Matt delt the next hand. On the bet he flipped the next card to each player. A bet was made and then raised. Buster and Barry folded. Russell and Brett were still in. Matt flipped the next card to Brett, Russell, and was ready to deal him self.

"Hold it right there Matt," Russell ordered.

Matt froze.

"What's wrong?" He responded.

"Nothing unless that card your about to deal your self is a King of Diamonds," Russell warned. "Now slowly flip that card over as so everyone here can see."

Matt hesitated for a long ten seconds, then went for his gun.

Russell's .44 belched out an ear shattering bang with flame blowing and burning a hole into Matt's chest, sending him and his chair over on its back.

"Buster, turn that next card," Russell ordered.

Buster reached over and turned the card. "King of Diamonds," he whispered not believing what he saw.

Russell holstered his pistol, scraped up his winnings; put them in his vest pocket.

"I guess I won't be coming out for that job Brett," he remarked.

Someone yelled, "Get the sheriff."

"He's out of town 'til tomorrow afternoon," the bartender responded.

Relief hit Russell, but he knew he would have to leave in the morning.

Just then a man walked in demanding what happened.

Bart looked up at the acting deputy and reported, "Self defense Bill. This here man caught that one," pointing to the dead man on the floor. "Cheating, and when he confronted him he went for his gun, and lost."

"What's your name son?" Bill asked Russell.

"John, John Tillman," Russell answered.

"Well mister Tillman, don't plan on leaving town without giving a statement to the sheriff. He'll be back some time tomorrow afternoon," he warned.

"What ever you say," Russell promised. "Can I go now I'm tired and don't feel good about killing a man," lying again.

Some of what he said was true. He did go to his room and go to sleep.

The next day the town seemed normal. Russell headed for the livery stable and saddled his horse. He put his saddle bags and bed role on and walked to the door. Looking around he saw that the deputies' horse was gone. He checked his gun lifting it from the holster and sliding it easy back in.

Leading his horse he walked over to the bank and wrapped the rein once over the pole bar.

Entering the bank with his saddle bags he noticed only a few patrons doing business. He pulled his gun and announced, "My name is Russell Hillman and this is a hold up. Fill these with money, keep your mouth shut and no one will get shot, any funny business and you will."

The clerks went to work and filled the bags as fast as they could. Out of the corner of his eye he saw a man slowly going for his gun. The next thing was Russell's gun spitting a bullet into the man's side, sending him to the floor. Grabbing the saddle bags he shot one of the clerks for no reason.

Running outside he jumped on his horse and high tailed it to the east. Once out of town he turned north like he had a posse on his heels. He rode fast and hard 'til he thought his horse was going to give out then brought him to a walk. He searched the hills for a possible place to hide out for a while. Once he got to a heavily wooded area high on a hill where he could almost see a full three hundred and sixty degrees he stopped and dismounted to rest the horse. He would rest for a few hours before continuing if the coast was clear. This was not new to him, he knew how to slip the law and get out clean.

Once settled he checked the saddle bags to how well he did. He counted almost seven thousand dollars, a lot more than he had figured on, a heck of a lot more. Thinking how this would drive the reward up for Russell Hillman, bank robber and killer.

A slight smile appeared on his face realizing his reputation was growing.

CHAPTER 8

Jeb and Vince came into town for a social visit. Vince wanted to hand out cigars to Jebs acquaintances or to anyone for that matter being a proud father of a baby boy. When they walked into the saloon and got word of the robbery and killings it all of a sudden didn't seem all that important to Vince. Not that it wasn't, but the death of innocent people trying to do they're job being shot down in cold blood, with Matt being the exception, well that didn't fit too well with Vince or Jeb. He could hand out cigars anytime. Right know he wanted to know more of the killing.

"Yes sir, he robbed the bank and gave his real name before he took off, Russell Hillman," the bartender reported.

"The sheriff put a pose together but figures he had too much of a head start on them," another man continued.

"Russell Hillman," Jeb retorted. "What direction he leave town?"

"East," the man answered.

"That name mean anything to you?" Vince asked.

"It means a lot. I'm surprised you don't recognize it," Jeb responded. "This guy's a gunfighter wanted in over four states. I've heard the sheriff speak of him before. The man he shot in the bank was a friend of mine and the teller I talked to often when I did my banking. They were two good men and never would have had a chance had they pulled on him. I need to ride out and join the pose," Jeb announced.

"If you know anyone who can stay with Jane I'll go with you," Vince offered.

"Maybe Ben Johnson's wife could stay with her, but it's not your fight, you needn't go," Jeb said.

"If these men were friends of yours then they were friends of mine, so it makes it my business just as much as hunting the rustlers." Vince barked out.

"Ok, let's ride out to see Ben and see if his wife can help," Jeb responded.

Riding up to the ranch house Vince saw Ben's place reminded him of his dad's spread. The layout was almost identical as though the two were built off the same plans. Ben met them on the porch as they rode up.

"You must be coming from town. Charlie was here a bit ago and told us what happened. Two of his hands were there when this John Tilman killed that card cheat," he announced.

"You haven't heard the latest?" Jeb asked.

"There's more?" Ben asked.

'The man's real name is Russell Hillman, he robbed the bank killing Smitty and one of the tellers as he left," Jeb reported.

"Damn, not Smitty. Oh my God, he never hurt anyone. Has the wife and those three kids," Ben said with concern. "Russell Hillman, huh? I've heard that name. Has a reputation all over the territory, quite a bounty on him to."

"That's him," Jeb replied.

"Ben, we came to ask a favor. Vince and I want to go meet-up with the pose. Do you think Karen could watch over Jane or check in on her from time to time?" Yes of course Ben answered. "I'll ask, but I'm sure she wouldn't mind."

"We're heading back to get our gear and will be heading out within the hour," Jeb responded. "Thanks Ben, we owe you."

Vince and Jeb reined the horses around and spurred the horses heading back to the ranch.

Back at the ranch Vince explained to Jane what they were up to. She wasn't really receptive to the idea but knew there was no way to talk them out of it.

"You two be careful and come back in one piece, promise," she said with concern.

Within the hour they were heading East at a fast gallop. They had a lot of ground to make up to catch up with the pose. Jeb knew the pose would have to slow to track Hillman giving them time to catch up. They were about a half day ride out Jeb figured.

They had gotten off to a late start; darkness was closing in on them fast. A full moon was giving them a few more hours to travel, possibly all night.

The pose stopped setting up camp knowing it would be dangerous if they were getting anywhere close to Hillman. Not wanting to warn him off they decided to wait and start out at dawn.

Vince and Jeb rode throughout the night. In the early dawn they could see men walking their horses about a half mile ahead. They knew they had caught up with the posse. The men all stopped as they noticed the two riding up on them.

"Glad you could join us Jeb." The sheriff praised, looking over at Vince.

"That's Ok Sheriff, Smitty was a friend of mine. I want to see this Hillman fella hang as much as you," Jeb answered. "I knew the teller just to talk to, but he deserves just as much justice."

"The tracks look as if he high-tailed it up those hills over yonder. It would give him almost a full three hundred and sixty degree view. We need to be real careful; I don't want anyone getting shot." The sheriff warned. "Jack you take two men and circle around to the left, Johnny you take two others and go off to the right."

Russell was no fool taking careful aim at the sheriff squeezing the trigger at the same time. When the rifle belched out it took only seconds to see the sheriff fall back off his horse. Looking in disbelief all members of the pose froze. Seeing not only their sheriff lying there on the ground dead he was also their friend.

Jack yelled out, "Let's get em men," leading the attack straight up the hill.

He was the next one to fall back out of his saddle as the thunder from Russell's rifle sounded.

Russell mounted his horse and raced down the back side of the hill. It was only a couple of minutes to reach the bottom where he had sighted a dry wash which shielded him from sight and again had a good lead on his pursuers. It took the pose twice that long since it was such a sharp incline they were trying to conquer. They slowed and cautiously reached the top only to discover their killer had vanished.

Having a clear view of the territory they saw nothing.

Jeb held back Vince, "Come with me, I have a idea," racing off along the base of the mountain.

Colt was no slouch when it came to running which surprised Vince to see how Jebs horse held his own on the lead. They raced almost three miles when they came to a break to the left leading them to the direction Russell had taken. In just a few minutes they reached the wash noticing the dust Russell's horse was making. Just moments before he was coming around a bend, Jeb asked Vince to stay put as he dismounted and ran down into the wash. Russell racing around the bend not believing his eyes when he saw Jeb standing alone in the middle of the dry wash.

The wash may have given Hillman protection from the posse but it sure didn't hide the sound of hooves crashing down on the rocks at a full run.

Pulling back on the reins bringing his horse to a stop Russell jumped down to meet his challenger.

"Go for your gun or drop it," Jeb ordered.

Russell a man of few words and knowing if he had any chance to clear the path for his escape it had to be now. He went for his gun.

Both guns belched out thunder almost simultaneously. Both men were standing starring at each other. Jebs gun was the next thing heard with Russell's firing into the dirt a split second after. Russell took the second shot dead in the chest. Jeb looked up to Vince, his face white as a ghost.

What had just happened people talked or read about but rarely witnessed. Both men had missed with their first shot. The victor was the one who realized it first and took the second shot and making it count.

Vince and Jeb stared at each other for quite a few seconds finding no words to say. Jeb saw Vince with his gun out pointing in the direction of Russell. Russell was in a no win situation not even realizing it.

Jeb went to slip his gun back into the holster only to find it wouldn't go. Looking down he saw where a .44 bullet had deformed it. The two men were about ten feet too far away from each other. Russell had fanned his gun before he had it leveled pulling it to the left and low at his target hitting Jebs holster. Jeb must have done the same but missed his target. He immediately taking the second shot and making it count.

The pose was rounding the turn finding the chase was over.

Pulling up to a stop the leader yelled to the rest, "Jeb shot Russell Hillman. He was supposed to be the best."

"He was that," Jeb started to confess.

"Jeb, let it go," Vince yelled out, "Let's get home."

Jeb climbed up the bank to get to Vince and his horse. Looking up to Vince as he stuck a foot in the stirrup to climb up, he noticed Vince with his head down shaking it and chuckling.

"You take the cake friend, I thought you were a dead man," Vince admitted.

"I'm not superstitious buddy, but I do believe you do have a guardian angel watching over you," Vince conceded.

"Well I do, but it just occurred to me, who's watching over our cattle while we're all out here miles away from the ranch?" He responded. "Let's get back, pronto. By the looks of those clouds coming we're in for a hell of a storm. Let them bring the bodies back to town."

Reining their horses around, they spurred them to a full gallop and headed home.

CHAPTER 9

Looking up to the sky as they were leaving the saloon, Jack looked over to Frank, giving him a slap on his back.

"Frank, let's get the gang. The pose's out searching the mountain side for that killer. Looks like it's gonna rain, leaving us opportunity to get us about one hundred head," Jack snickered.

"They went east, and we'll be going south. How much better opportunity could we ask for? We should have the cattle delivered and be back in plenty of time for an alibi. Let's get," Frank said. "The bartender knows we were here today, we should be back before dark tomorrow. We need to come straight back for some card playing."

"Now you're thinking smart, partner," Jack answered.

Mounting their horses they high-tailed it out to meet the gang. They made sure to walk the horses to the edge of town, then spurred them like all get out.

Pulling up to the cabin they could see horses tied, knowing that all the men were inside and accounted for. Sober enough to ride and get the plan straight, Frank hoped.

The rain was now starting as they dismounted and went in. Instructing the men to which ranch they would hit, how they would pair-up to break away about sixty head.

Planning to meet up at the south bend of the Continental Divide where another group would take the cattle. By doing this it kept the first group in the dark of where the cattle were taken, so if confronted by the law they could enforce their innocence of not knowing anything.

The men saddled their horses and headed for the three different ranches. The weather was in their favor so the faster they could round up the strays and get to the bend of the mountain, the faster they could return without leaving much chance of any clues, providing the rain lasted long enough to cover all tracks.

It only took a few hours for each pair to have their cattle cut, herded, and heading in a heavy rain for the assigned rendezvous. Their instructions were to leave the cattle and return to the ranch together. Anyone who stayed behind would be shot on site.

During the night the herd was taken to an undisclosed area where another group of men would take over. This is when the cattle would mysteriously vanish and never be seen again. On their return to the outskirts of town most of the men of the first group returned to their homes while others went on into town to make their presence known, establishing an alibi.

Vince and Jeb rode up to the house only to be greeted to the barrel of a .44-40 pointing at them.

"Oh Vince, Jeb, am I glad you're back, I've been so scared," Jane said shaking.

"What happened?" Vince asked jumping down from Colt.

"Three men came to the door knocking, telling me to open. I told them to go away, that I had a gun and knew how to use it. I brought it to the window to show them I wasn't kidding," She responded. "They told me that they were going to come in and show me how a lady should be treated. Anyone that would leave a lady alone and go off didn't deserve a woman like me. I told them if they took one step forward or said another word I would shoot. I was scared Vince, I knew if they crashed through the door I couldn't shoot all of them before one of them would get to me. They hung out for a while but I think they were too scared to chance it and rode off."

"Can you describe these men or the horses they rode?" Vince asked.

"I'll never forget them or their horses," Jane responded.

As soon as she was done giving the descriptions to Vince he was on his horse headed for town.

Jeb reined his horse around to follow yelling, "Don't worry, I'll watch his back."

"Please do Jeb," Jane retorted.

Jeb knew there was going to be a gunfight leaving three men dead in just a short time. He was tired but he figured he could put off sleep a little longer hoping one of the three would know of the cattle rustling. By him being there, he may be able to help one stay alive long enough to spill his guts.

The ride into town seemed short as mad as Vince was. His mind was going over what could have happened to Jane and the baby while he was out playing pose. Those men killed at the bank were Jebs friends, he knew Jeb would have caught up with the pose and been alright. He should have stayed with Jane.

Vince went through the bat wings like a bull. He stopped and scoped the room, taking in all the faces searching for the three Jane described. Off to the right he saw three men with their eyes wide opened, like a fox caught in a hen house. These were definitely the three Jane described. Jeb walked in behind him stopping next to him.

"You three, stand up," Vince ordered.

Two of the three were Frank and Jack, the other Vince never saw before.

The unidentified man stood first letting his hand hang low to his gun. Frank and Jack followed.

"Your pretty good scaring a young lady, how are you with a man?" Vince challenged. "You seem to want trouble with me. Now you found it."

Frank and Jack knew what was to happen next. The third man they were with was a hired gun leaving them feeling pretty confident. The three spread out making themselves a harder target.

The third man when for his gun with Frank and Jack following his move.

Vince shot the unknown man as his gun fired into the floor. Vince's second shot took out Frank before he cleared leather. Jeb shot Jack in the shoulder as he was bringing his gun up. The two Vince shot were dead. Jack was on the floor trying to pick up his gun but both Vince and Jeb knew he couldn't with his shoulder wound so stood there with their guns on him.

From the side of them the roar of a gun went off. Vince and Jeb turn to shoot but instantly saw the shooter had his gun pointing to Jack. They then looked back at Jack to see him lying dead, bleeding profusely.

"He was going for his gun," the shooter yelled, "you all saw it."

"We needed him alive," Jeb yelled back. "He couldn't have picked up his gun with his shoulder wounded like that. We needed him alive."

"Some gratitude, I just saved your life," the man yelled.

"This was none of your affair, I should shoot you," Jeb yelled.

"No ones gonna do anymore shooting," the deputy yelled as he burst though the batwings hearing everything.

"This man just shot Jack, who could have given us some answers to some questions to what's happening around here," Jeb pleaded.

"That's right," Vince added.

"Deputy, the man was going for his gun, I shot him saving these two ungrateful men," he responded in his defense.

Just then Vince let loose with a smashing right fist to the man's chin sending him crashing over chairs and smashing through a table, knocking him out cold.

43

"Stop it, I mean now!" The deputy yelled. "I want you two in my office right now. We'll sort it out there."

"It was clearly self defense deputy. I'll vouch for these two," a patron said.

"That's right, that there man had no right shooting Jack again, it was none of his affair," another man butt in.

"Ok, you two bring that one to the jail when he comes to," the deputy ordered.

"Sure will," the two answered.

When the men entered the office Sam the deputy fell into his chair lost for words. He just lost his boss and a good friend while trying to apprehend Russell Hillman.

"Jeb, mind pouring three coffees?" Sam asked, pointing over to the wood stove.

"Can anyone tell me what's going on here? I've lost three men and my boss this week. Now I'm sitting here with another friend and a man I don't even know. There are three dead men in the saloon and a man being brought to me for I don't know what. Jeb, talk to me. Please explain what's going on here."

Jeb took a long swallow from his cup. "I don't know anything about this Russell Hillman, Sam. I know he killed a good friend of mine so I felt obligated to go along to help apprehend him, but I had no idea it would play out the way it did. While we were out chasing Hillman it occurred to me no one was watching the ranches and had a feeling something was going to go down when it started to rain. When we got home we found out that Vince's wife was harassed by the three men that were at the saloon. They figured on pulling guns rather than taking a beating. We didn't want to kill anyone, but it was them or us. I wounded one so we could possibly get some information from him about the missing cattle. That's when this guy comes up from behind and does him in giving us some damn fool story he was going for his gun. I think this man being brought in is up to his ears to what's going on. It will be up to you to get information out of him. Pressure him, tell him he's going to hang if he doesn't talk. Scare him anyway you can. I know he knows something. This is our first big break to find out about the missing cattle."

Sam looked over to Vince, "What's your part in all this? Who are you?

Jeb took over, "His name is Vince Rodgers," he lied, "He's a good friend of mine from Arkansas. He and his wife are staying with me. While he's here he offered to help me find who's behind the rustling of Slocomb's, Barnett's, and my cattle. We were to get together and meet one evening to sort things out when this Hillman guy came tearing into town robbing and killing."

Vince wasn't too keen on Jeb lying about his name but knew why he did it. He hoped it wouldn't come back to bite him in the future.

"We'll Vince Rodgers, I hope you don't mind if I wire to check on you. Would you?" Sam asked.

"I have nothing to hide, do what you need to do. Like Jeb said I'm staying with him 'til we can get the men responsible for taking his and his neighbors cattle," Vince conceded.

Just then the door opened and two men pushed a third into the room.

Sam got his keys walked back to the cells ordering the men to put him in one then locked him in.

"What's your name? Who are you working for?" Sam asked the prisoner.

He could only whisper, "I'm Tom Reycon,"

Sam knew he was probably drunk and still delirious from the punch Vince administered to him back at the saloon.

"We'll talk in the morning," Sam said turning heel walking back out to the office.

"If you don't need us any more we'd like to get back to the ranch," Jeb asked.

"Us too," the two others said.

"Go ahead, there isn't anything more can be done here," Sam admitted.

Sam was ready to turn the lights down since everyone had left when he heard Reycon stir. He had fallen off the cot and had thrown up from being nauseous from the hit Vince had administered. Sam wanted to go home but felt he should get Reycon back on his cot keeping him from lying in his own vomit.

"Who was the third man who was shot tonight," Sam asked as he lifted him back onto the cot.

"Jake Ballard," Reycon answered as he rolled over and passed out.

Once they were on they're way out of town Vince rode up next to Jeb.

"I know what you did for me back there but I just know it's gonna come back to bite me," he said with concern. "I'm gonna go back tomorrow and let Sam know the truth."

"Why don't we let it go for now. He probably will forget to check on you anyway. If he does I'll let him know why I did it," Jeb promised. "We'll be getting a new sheriff in the weeks to come. If you still feel you need to tell your real name you can do it then."

Riding along for a bit in silence, he felt Jeb was right. There was no reason to let any information out any sooner than needed.

"I know that Reycon knows something he's not telling," Jeb said. "I want to make sure he doesn't get out without Sam pressing some kind of confession or at least telling who he works for. This has been going on too long. Like Ben said, it won't be long before they have to sell out and move on like my brothers. What they did to Jane just isn't gonna be tolerated either. But I guess you proved that to the whole town just a while ago."

"I think Reycon killed Jack to keep him quiet about something alright, but I think it goes deeper than just that fella in jail. I hope he wires around checking his back ground more extensively than mine." Vince replied with some concern in his voice. I hope Jane's alright. I hope she doesn't get cold feet and want to leave."

"She's a strong woman, I'm sure she'll be just fine," Jeb said reassuring

Riding up to the house Jane came out holding the baby, "Please tell me your both alright," she said with concern looking them both over for any signs of injury.

"We're fine honey but the three men that harassed you won't be giving trouble to anyone else again," Vince confessed.

"Oh no! You didn't kill them, my God please say you didn't kill them," she pleaded.

"Jane, it was them or us," Jeb announced, "There was a third man in jail for questioning. We'll need to go back to town in the morning to meet with the sheriff and see how much this other fella knows. Dinner ready? I'm starved."

"Yes, I hope you like fried chicken and potatoes with sweet corn. Brett's wife Betty brought vegetables figuring now that there's a lady around you men should eat right," she responded.

"Sounds fantastic!" Jeb answered. "Better watch it, I may get used to this home cookin' and have to keep ya here."

Hearing that Jane wasn't too concerned about what happened earlier in the day.

After dinner they sat around the table with a last mug of coffee complementing Jane on her cooking.

"I could live on fried chicken," Jeb announced.

"Me too," Vince admitted.

It had been a long day for the two. Thinking of bed with a full stomach sure sounded good. Jane had other ideas.

"Can we go sit out on the porch and will you play the guitar? I found in the living room corner Jeb? You do play don't you?" Jane asked with hope.

"For you, anything pretty lady," he surrendered.

Not only could he play, he could play very well. He played, they sang, making all the bad things that happened that day disappear for the moment. The moon was shining full for a change. A comfortable breeze helped pass the time without letting the lateness spoil the good time they were sharing. Finally after finishing a song he laid the guitar down, surrendering to his tiredness.

"I'm going to excuse myself and hit the hay," Jeb surrendered. "It's gonna be a long day tomorrow. Good night all."

Vince and Jane answered in harmony, "Night Jeb, see ya at breakfast."

Jane and Vince stayed out a while longer. Vince knew he owed that much to Jane. He had been spending so much time with Jeb he was scared she may think he was ignoring her. Jeb could hear some whispering from the two but knew it wasn't anything to do with him and was out like a light within minutes.

Jane wanting Vince in her arms, asked Vince to take her to bed and comfort her. It was late now and both were exhausted.

Looking over to Vince she could see his face even with the lantern turned at its lowest. "Honey, I'm confused, we've not been here a week yet and already you've been in a gunfight. Is this where you really want to settle down? It's as if the baby and I aren't even here. You've been off with Jeb almost every day. I'm lonely for you honey.

I thought you were going to leave everything behind when we came out here to find Jeb. I need a husband and Richard needs a father. Maybe I should have stayed back with my sister. I know what Jeb means to you and I appreciate you trying to help him but there are other ranchers here that can help Jeb too. I want you to be here for me and the baby more often, I need you near me. I can fend for myself in times of danger but I was really scared today when you weren't here for us. I have Richard to think of, it's not just you and me anymore. Talk to me Vince, I'm your wife and the mother of your child. I need to know what's on your mind. When is this going to be over so we can be a family with our own home?" She said with tears in her eyes knowing she was being selfish but on the other hand feeling abandoned.

Vince laid there silent a moment to make sure he would say the right things.

"I'm so sorry for making you feel this way. I owe Jeb my life and promised to help solve this problem that the territory is experiencing. Up to now no one, not even the sheriff has had even a clue. Today we had a break through and I think things are going to come to a head. Arrests will be made. I promise you we will make a decision together about where we want to live out our lives. Until then I promise you I'll stay around more often for you and Richard," he promised. "Jeb will understand, he's that kind of a friend. You know that."

"I love you Vince, I don't know what I'd do without you. Please be careful," she pleaded.

"You know I will. I don't want anything to happen to me either. Go to sleep love," he whispered.

CHAPTER 10

The morning came fast. The three were just finishing breakfast when they heard a rider coming up the trail. Who ever it was, he was coming at break neck speed. Jeb grabbed his rifle and was out on the porch the same time the rider's horse was hitting the skids.

Johnny was one of the men that rode with the pose hunting Hillman, now he was skidding his horse up to the front porch spurting out the news he was sent to deliver.

"Reycon's dead, found him this morning in his cell with a knife stuck in him. They say it's a knife of a Cheyenne. Must of come in the middle of the night and shucked him through the barred window in the back. Sam said he never heard no ruckus, yet when he brought breakfast in for Reycon this morning he found him bled to death right there on the floor. Sam said I should get out here and tell you fellas."

"You had much trouble with Indians lately?" Vince asked Jeb.

"Not that I've heard of. I've heard of tribes migrating north. Sioux or Arapaho's I could believe but not the Shoshone or Pawnee.

"I think we need to get to town and see Sam. If there hasn't been any trouble with Indians in the past why would it start now? Something's not adding up," Vince mentioned.

Vince and Jeb saddled the horses while Johnny waited and then they rode into town together.

Tying the horses to the tie bar in front of the jail, Jeb and Johnny headed for the door of the sheriffs office.

"I'll be right with you," Vince said turning heel spanning the area with a cautious look.

Jeb and Johnny entered the office while Vince walked out to the back of the jail. Again he fanned the area with caution then started to inspect the ground just below the window of the jail cells. Squatting down, he inspected the ground finding the one thing he expected. Prints made by two different pairs of boots. He kept looking to make sure, but his findings doubt if Indians were involved. There would be foot prints of moccasins. He double and triple checked but still found only the boot prints of white men. The knife used was only used to throw off the investigation and to pin the crime on Indians. Whoever killed Reycon did it to prevent him from talking. Reycon must not have been a very trusting man, Vince thought. What ever the case, Vince needed to bring Sam to the back of the jail to show him what he missed and clear the threat against the Indians.

Sam agreed with Vince as did Johnny and Jeb after seeing what Vince showed them. The boot sizes looked about the same size with one pair making a more distinct mark meaning one of the killers was a heavier man than the other.

"This was clearly a set up," Sam said. "I guess I should have come back here myself earlier."

Vince thought to himself and understood why Sam was only acting as sheriff 'til one could be appointed putting Sam back as deputy.

"Sam, did you ever get the name of the third man's name from Reycon that was shot last night?" Vince asked inquisitively.

"Jake Ballard," Sam replied. "That's the name he gave me last night after everyone left."

Vince's mouth almost dropped to the floor.

"Vince, what's wrong, you look like you just saw a ghost, you're completely white. You ok?" Jeb asked with concern.

"I know a Jake Ballard. He also has a brother Mike. They grew up in the same town as I did. They were trouble then so I'd expect no different of them now. But what are the chances of them being here in Alamos as me?" Vince replied with some confusion in his voice. "Do you know of a Mike Ballard living in the territory Sam?"

"Can't say that I do," Sam answered, "But I didn't know of Jake 'til I spoke to Ben. If he does have a brother he could be living right here, near-by, under an alias.

Vince thought for a second realizing that he just heard something come out of Sam's mouth that sounded half like a real sheriff would say. Maybe there was hope for this man after all. If Mike was in the territory working with his brother how was he ever to find out. Even if he walked right past him, would he recognize him? It was years since he saw either of them.

"Where's Jake's body? I want to look at him," Vince asked.

"Down at the undertaker's. Probably being fitted, if not already nailed in a pine box."

Vince was out the door in a flash heading down the street. If he was to pull out every nail he would, just to get another look at Jake.

"Where's the fire?" Jeb asked, as he caught up to his friend.

"I need to see him again. See if I recognize him now that I know who he is. Jog my memory, then maybe I'll remember Mike if I should run into him," Vince replied.

"I just shot his brother, I don't think you're gonna have to look very hard to find him. He could have his sights on us as we speak," Jeb answered with concern.

When they turned the corner there was a box open with a body waiting for the cover to be nailed in place. Vince walked over and took a look. Other than being so dead pale he recognized him immediately. Thinking back to the fight he and his brother Cal had with the brothers was as if it just happened yesterday. He was now convinced he'd have no trouble recognizing Mike.

Vince hurried back to the sheriff's office.

"Sam, wire all the territorial sheriff's office's and see if there's any warrants for these Ballard brothers. Give them a good description in case they're running under aliases. Then we need to get it in all the papers that Jake Ballard was killed and see if that will draw his brother out. He could be the leader of the outfit that's been rustling the cattle," Vince stated. "We may want to hurry in case Mike thinks the heat coming down on him and he decides to leave town."

Vince could only hope he would come face to face with Mike Ballard. To him he still had a score to settle with him, even if it was years back. This time it would be legal and Vince would make sure Mike made the first move to prove it self defense. He and Jeb went over to the saloon for a beer before heading back to the ranch. The bartender had their beers poured already as they eased up to the bar.

"How many men you two shoot up today?" the barkeep teased.

"I rightly don't see the humor if you don't mind." Vince remarked.

"Sorry, I guess that was pretty uncalled for," he admitted. "I apologize; the beers are on the house to make up for my smart mouth."

"That won't be necessary; anyone can put their foot in their mouth every now and then. Heck, if I had to by a beer for every time I've done it I'd be plumb broke," Vince admitted.

After drinking up the beers Vince put his mug down.

"I told Jane I'd stay around the ranch more often. We better head back before she starts doubting my word."

It would have been nice to stay for a few more but Vince didn't feel right after just hours ago making a promise like that to Jane. The weather was real nice and the two kinda dogged their way back to the ranch. Arriving up to the house Jane was out on the porch with the baby, not necessarily waiting for the men but taking advantage of the nice weather.

"We'll hello fellas, how about a nice glass of lemonade?" Jane asked.

"Don't mind if we do," Jeb replied.

Jane went into the house to get the men the drinks and the two took seats on the porch to stretch out and relax.

"Jeb, I've been thinking," Vince started. "What if Jake Ballard was using an alias name and didn't realize he gave his real name as he was dying? I'm thinking his brother could be right here in the territory and be running a rustling business. I'm thinking also they may have given up a clue now that it's been proven the Indians are innocent. We need to go to town tonight and see if anyone mentions the names of the three we shot last night. We know Frank and Jack but we need to see if anyone mentions a name other than Jake. My bet is we will. Then we'll need to find his brother, probably using an alias. Find him and we may get to the bottom of how this operation has been working."

Jane came out with a pitcher and glasses. The rest of the afternoon excluded anymore talk of the Ballards and focused on Jane and Richard. This was how Vince had hoped to come out to visit his friend and knew Jane felt the same way. Vince made sure he gave Jane his undivided attention in order to get to go into town later with Jeb without getting too much flack. It seemed that Richard was growing at a phenomenal rate. Vince was looking forward to teaching him the thing his dad had taught him and his siblings. It would be a while before the baby even took his first steps. Sitting there he thought how nice it would have been to have his family there to share the enjoyment of watching Richard grow. For now he needed to help his friend and hoped it would soon be over, but he knew from past experience not to get his hopes up. Later Jane and the baby went in for a nap. Vince found this a good time to go behind the barn out of sight and practice with his pistols in order to stay sharp.

Chapter 11

"We delivered the last of the cattle; it's time to move on. Too many mistakes are going to bring the heat down on us and it's only a matter of time before it all leads back to me. That I won't have," came a voice from the head of the table. "We've wore out our welcome in this here town."

"I say we take care of Jeb and his friend for all the trouble they've caused," one of the other men said directing it to the man who just spoke.

"And who's gonna do that?" The voice came back. "Three men tried and three men died. You want to be next? No I say let's pick up stakes and get. I'll take care of those two personally another time."

"You're the boss, but if the opportunity should arrive I'll take care of the two for you," the man promised.

"Get out of town and stay out of town, both of you, do you hear? I don't want my head in no noose because of two gun crazed men. I've paid the rest and they're gone. I'll have your money later tonight and you can get out of the territory as fast as your horses can carry you," ending the conversation.

The two men left the cabin but it was pretty clear once they got their money they would stay or leave on their terms and nobody would tell them different.

"I'm tired of being told what to do. Maybe I like this town. Nobody expects us of any wrong doing. Maybe we will lay low let the boss clear the territory and maybe get our own business going with the cattle. There's still a lot of money to be made. Why not cash in on a few more runs then get out? What do you think cousin?" the man asked.

The two cousins Matt and Steve had been hiring out to many rustlers from time to time but Matt knew now how much money was to be made. Why work for someone else for gravy when you can have the meat and potatoes too. It was their time to start on their own. They knew where to get the cattle since the ranches were all so familiar now.

The weather had been holding fast, nice and comfortable. It hadn't rained in a few days and the moon had been shinning bright. A slight breeze was making sleeping even nice. Knowing that the weather couldn't hold-out forever now would be the time to scope out the herds, and then wait it out until the rains came, get the cattle and get out. Matt had it all figured out too well. What Matt didn't know was what to do with the cattle when they got them down to the valley. That was always taken care of for them.

"Well I don't know about you but I'm going into town after we get paid for some drinks and play some cards," Matt said.

"I don't know Matt. You heard what the boss said," cautioned Steve.

"After we get paid we have no boss. So like I said I'm going to town," answered Matt sarcastically.

Steve rode along-side not saying a word. He knew Matt was one that could get into a confrontation with a man with little reason. This worried him.

Later that afternoon the two went back to collect the money owed to them. When they rode-up they could sense something was wrong.

"Wait here Steve," warned Matt as he was dismounting. "I'll take a look."

He walked up to the door and noticed it was cracked open a bit. He cautiously pushed it fully open only to discover it abandon.

"Steve, you better come take a look for yourself. You ain't gonna like this," Matt announced.

Steve got down and walked in to see what Matt had just discovered. He kicked a box that was sitting on the floor.

"That skunk!" Matt yelled. "I'll kill him for this. I will find him and I will kill him. He's gone, our money is gone!"

"Maybe he went to town to meet up with us," Steve said wishfully.

"You're as gullible as you look to think something like that," Matt yelled. "You can see he's cleared out which means he panicked and left while the leaving was good. Come on let's get into town just in case your half right," running out to his horse.

They mounted and rode into town slowing as they hit the main street as not to attract any attention. Looking around for any mule wagon or horse but not seeing anything they pulled up to the saloon, dismounted and tied the horses. There didn't seem to be many men in the saloon as expected. Usually after a shooting it took a few days for men to start coming back.

Walking through the bat doors they saw they had their pick of seating. Finding a place off to the side with their backs to the walls, they ordered drinks. What men were in there were of no interest to the two so they kicked back and drank, waiting. What they didn't know but were sure they'd spot if it happened to come through those two doors.

"Getting the cattle herded won't be a problem," Steve stated. "But we don't have the connection we need to deliver and collect."

"Let me take care of that, just keep your eyes and ears open and we may find all the answers we need right here, tonight," Matt replied.

As time went by the place started getting busier with men settling up against the bar while others settled in at tables for some drinking and card playing. Even the piano started to fill the air with all the familiar tunes the player knew and played every night. It was still early with the smoke from cigarettes and cigars stating to close-off the visibility to the patrons. Consumption of alcohol would soon make the air more tolerable.

It wasn't long before a couple of men asked Matt and Steve if they could pull a chair and get a card game going. For the next few hours they played, winning enough money to help get their minds off the money they were swindled out of. This was good but Matt was the one that had no intentions of letting it go no matter how much he raked in. He was quite a card player who had made his living gambling before getting caught up with the cattle rustling. That only happened when he met and liked Steve who was a better thief than a card player. The chairs emptied and refilled with other men as the evening past. Matt rolled his winnings several times hiding the money in his vest pocket not wanting to advertise his success. Steve was having a pretty good string of luck him self. Matt kept notice of who came through the doors often with hopes of two things; one being the man owing them the money should walk in or two; someone came in mentioning names of who might know how to get rid of stolen cattle.

It was getting pretty late and time was running out. Other than his luck at the table Matt was getting nervous that this would be a wasted night when two men made a grand entrance in a loud and obnoxious manner. Walking up to the bar laughing and slapping each other on the back they yelled for a full bottle of whiskey from the barkeep. Two gold coins made quite the noise as the bottle and glasses were set down. The one spanned the room looking for a place to sit. Matt kicked an empty chair out and told one of the other men at the table to get lost. He was losing his patience and was grabbing at straws but had no intentions of losing out on any chance of gaining information he and Steve were looking for. The whiskey was being downed like water with Matt encouraging them without raising suspicion.

"You two look like you've had a prosperous day. Been prospecting?" Matt asked looking down at some gold coins on the table to continue the card game.

"Nope just finished a job ram-rodding a bunch of cattle from the south," one of the men answered. "My names Trip and my friend here's Tom."

"Matt and Steve," Matt replied nodding his head at Steve.

"Glad to meet you fellas, what's your game?" looking down at the cards.

"Five Card Stud," Steve replied, throwing down some bills to get the hand going.

"I think we can do better than that," Trip replied sliding in a twenty dollar gold piece.

"That's pretty gutsy of you on your first hand ain't it friend?" Matt asked.

"Tell ya in just a few minutes," he and Tom laughing.

"We'll tone it down, after all it's your table," Tom replied.

"I'll tell ya in just a few minutes," Matt answered in a sarcastic way.

In just a few hands and some betting there was a four hundred dollar pot in the middle of the table. Being the first hand Matt was instantly suspicious of what was going down.

"Call," Steve ordered, seeing this was getting out of control.

Matt threw down three Jacks knowing that was a pretty good hand. Steve threw his cards face down in disgust. Tom threw his in face down following Steve.

"We'll let's see em," Matt challenged.

Trip threw his cards face up; three sevens.

Matt was reaching prematurely for the pot when Trip threw his other two cards; two nines.

"Full house," he announced.

Matt didn't like what just happened but sat back in the chair and watched Trip scrape up his winnings.

We'll play a bit more conservative here on out," he stated. "Beginners luck."

"I'll say, he hasn't won a first hand for quite a while," Tom answered.

Matt's suspicion was still there but Tom's statement cooled it off somewhat took some of it away. He'd just see how the next few hands went.

Trip lost hand after hand but was betting light and would throw his cards in if he had nothing. It looked like he was not doing well but that first hand was enough to play all night and still leave the table with a substantial amount. Then he started to bet a little higher and would take every third or fourth hand, starting to win again without raising suspicion. He too started to pocket money so the others couldn't track his winnings.

Mean-while Vince and Jeb walked in without being noticed as the others were so engrossed in their game. Sitting across the room they too sat with their backs to the wall, drinking their beer and observing what was going on. As the night went on, the tables started to vacate. While the cards were being shuffled Matt looked around the room spotting Jeb and Vince. Their eyes almost met in sync. Matt turned white not believing he let him self get so wrapped up with the cards not to notice the two to walk-in. He kicked Steve under the table and nodded over to Jeb and Vince.

"You know of any cattle drives heading north?" Trip asked.

"Why don't we meet up tomorrow and I'll see if there's anything going on," Matt replied as he stood to excuse himself. "Come on Steve we gotta get. It's been nice."

"Tomorrow then," Trip said.

He and Steve turned heel and walked for the door but not until giving a deadly glance over to Vince and Jeb.

After they were gone Vince walked over to the table.

"What you find out?" he asked.

"We were told to find them tomorrow to see if they knew of any cattle to be driven north," Trip answered.

"Make sure you find them and report back to me as soon as you learn something," Vince ordered as he threw a couple of gold pieces on the table.

Vince walked back to Jeb hoping he wasn't seen talking to Tom and Trip.

"We may have found our men," he reported to Jeb. We'll know more tomorrow.

"That was a pretty good idea you came up with, I have to give you credit for that," Jeb answered. "We've found all we're gonna for tonight. Let's get back to the ranch."

Steve and Matt were no sooner walking their horses when they heard a horse come up behind them. Suspiciously they turned and found themselves facing a stranger.

"Can we help you?" Matt asked in a nasty way.

"Depends," the stranger answered. "My name is Clifford, I just left the salon a few minutes before you. I couldn't help over-hearing some of your conversation with those other two fellas. I wanted to warn you. I don't think you want to get involved with them if you're the two men I think you are."

"And why not? We don't know you anymore than we know them," replied Matt.

"Because I think you two have been driving cattle down to the break in the mountain for the past four months and I know this because I was with the men that drove them from there to their destination," Clifford admitted.

"What about the men in the saloon?" Matt asked.

"I never saw or heard of them before. So unless you have, I'd be mighty cautious what you say or show them," Clifford cautioned. "I got short handed over the last drive and I'm after the man who stiffed me, but I never met him or even knew his name. I'm broke so I thought I'd drive some cattle myself. When I over heard you I knew you were involved and thought I'd join in on your action if I'm right."

"You must be telling the truth Clifford, 'cause me and Steve here was cut short of our pay too. We're gonna go after it too, but figured we'd run a few herds outta here. Meeting you is a real good thing because we don't have the connection with anyone who knew where to take them after we got them to the mountain break. That was our next assignment but I didn't know it would come riding right up to us," Matt explained. "What do we do with those two men in there? How do we know if they're for real?"

"You don't, that's why I'm warning you. When you see them tomorrow bring them out to the cabin and I'll meet you and we'll see if they're for real or not," Clifford recommended.

"Sounds good to me, let's say we bring them to the cabin around eight tomorrow night," Matt suggested.

"I'll be there waiting. If we have to leave on a fast note it will be plenty dark for a safe getaway," Clifford admitted.

Chapter 12

Vince and Jeb got home to find Jane had already retired with the baby. Vince excused himself for the night and went to bed only to wake Jane as he climbed in next to her.

"I'm sorry honey, I didn't mean to wake you," Vince whispered.

"I'm glad your home," giving Vince a passionate kiss. "The babies been so good. I came in to lie down with him for just a few minutes and I guess I just fell hard to sleep. How did you make out in town?"

"I think we may have the best lead yet to find the rustlers. Hopefully in the next few days we can put an end to all this. But still no word on any Jake Ballard," Vince responded. "If he is part of this and still in the territory I'd think he'd make a move toward me or Jeb pretty darn soon. I'm beginning to have my doubts. I think if he was involved he's gone, letting money be more important than his own blood."

"Enough honey," as he rolled to her for her love.

Afterward Vince laid thinking, listening to a lone coyote and a far away hoot of an owl. It was hot with a small breeze to help make it bearable. He put his arms up and cupped his hands under his head. Jane's breathing brought relaxation to him, knowing everyone was safe. Then he shifted his thinking to the ranch back East and the events that lead him west. He knew right away he would be wakened by a nightmare this night. Every time he let his mind turn to the past he would wake from a nightmare.

Jane would be there to comfort him and make everything fine. Having her in his life was the best thing that ever happened to him with his son Robert, growing like a weed. Robert was now crawling giving Vince pleasure of watching him grow, doing something new every day. If he missed something Jane would be there to tell him when he arrived home. In a bit Vince fell off into sleep and was out for the night.

It was just a few hours when he woke finding his arms asleep, tingling under his head. He struggled to get them down to his sides. They were so sore from being up over his head for so long. Jane was still out, having her own dreams throughout the night. Now the night was still, a small breeze continued but the calls of the coyotes and owls were gone. Seeming like a few minutes, he woke to the smell of bacon and coffee. Jane was absent from the bed. He knew it was time to get up. Breakfast was waiting. He could hear voices out in the kitchen. Jeb was up with Robert and Jane. The warmth of the bed made it hard for Vince to get dressed. Sleeping under the sky in his bed roll was one thing but a good comfortable bed was hard to evacuate.

Everyone sat around the table enjoying the breakfast. Jeb was in heaven with all the service he had been getting, knowing that some day soon he would have to fend for himself again. Alone.

It was clouding up and looking pretty dreary. If it was going to rain these were the clouds that could be bet on.

"If it starts raining maybe we ought to split up and each run down to the herds to keep a look out. This seems to be when the cattle disappear," Jeb advised.

Just as he finished the thunder of horses hoofs were heard coming up to the ranch.

Jeb got up and checked out the window to find Charlie Smith, Ben Johnson along with Barry Slocomb and Brett Barnett their ranch hands.

Jeb opened the door. "Just in time for a fresh pot of coffee," he invited.

The four men quickly dismounted and tied the horses and proceeded to the front door.

"What brings you fellas out so early?" Jeb asked as Jane was serving cups of hot coffee to each the men.

"Well, it looks like the rains are closing in and seeing as we've gone such a spell without we figured it may hang for a while. This is when our cattle seem to disappear. Ben and I figured we should all get together and maybe put a plan together to catch us a cattle rustler or two," Charlie suggested.

"This is a coincidence, we were just talking about that at the table just minutes ago," Jeb confessed.

"Well, we have a feeling about this and that's why we brought Larry and Brett with us," Charlie said.

"I'll fetch a couple of my men so we can ride in pairs. We can cover much more ground that way," Jeb responded. "There were two men in the saloon last night trying to find a buyer or someone to take some cattle off their hands on a moments notice. I paid a couple of men to pose as cattlemen to see if we could flush any information out of them. They were supposed to make contact in town sometime today. Maybe if you sent Barry and Brett into town later they may over hear something, then we can make our own plan of attack when the time comes."

"How bout it boys? Can I count on you to nose around without raising suspicion?" Charlie asked.

"You know you can Charlie," Larry answered with sureness.

"Good. Get going and come back with some good news then," Charlie ordered.

"Come on Brett we got work to do," Larry announced.

They got up turned heel and were out the door in a flash, hooves pounding the ground as they left.

"Where do you want to meet up later?" Jeb asked Charlie.

"Ben's place would be fine. He's kinda the half way mark between us. Just hope we have something to report as not to waste anyone's time," he confessed.

"We're gonna have to do this on a trial and error, that's all. I wouldn't call it wasting time 'cause at least we're coming together as neighbors to get this thing done," Vince barked.

"Til then," the two ranchers stood and headed for the door. "Thanks for the coffee mam."

"Anytime, no bother at all. I like to see men working together. Much safer that way" Jane answered. "Maybe I can get my men back once this is over," she said with a smile.

Chapter 13

"Where are they?" Matt asked, running out of patience.

"They'll be here. There's too much money at stake not to," Steve answered.

"I hope your right. How many steer can we handle with four men?" Steve asked.

"I figured we'll push the limit seeing that it's our last job and having to split the money four ways about four hundred head ought to be enough to line our pockets 'til we can meet-up with that no good hombre that ran off with our money," Matt answered. "Get us a couple more beers here bartend."

The two got their beer and found a seat toward the back facing the batwings. Matt wanted privacy when they talked and security by facing the doors. Now it was time to wait and see who came.

It wasn't a half hour when the doors came open, but the two men that walked in weren't the two Matt and Steve were expecting.

Barry and Brett walked up to the bar seeing Matt and Steve out of the corner of their eyes and ordered two beers. They started small talk as if they had the day off and were just happy to drink the rest of the day away.

At first Matt got suspicious but when Tom and Tripp walked through the doors he kind of forgot about the other two. Watching them order themselves a beer and walk over to the table and seat themselves.

"Afternoon, men," Tripp said with a half smile on his face.

"Why the grin?" Matt asked, watching them suck down half their beers.

"No reason. Just hoping you have some good news for a couple of broke drovers," Tripp answered.

"Well we got the cattle," Matt lied. "So now we have to come to terms of what you can do for us and what you expect from it."

"How many cattle?" Tripp asked.

"Four hundred," he responded.

"Humm, how many men?" Tripp asked.

"Five," Matt answered.

"When?" Tripp asked.

"As soon as possible. Tomorrow or the next day. We'll be running them south, that's all I know for now," he reported.

Barry and Larry were continuing their conversation without a break, but they couldn't hear what was being said at the table not far from where they stood.

"We're to meet up with the ramrod of the herd outside town where we'll get our orders, so if you gentlemen will kindly finish your beers we'll be on our way," Matt announced.

They stood and left. Barry and Brett stood fast and finished another beer before heading out to report what they heard. They knew what they just found-out would be enough to make Charlie and Ben proud.

The weather was looking more like rain as the hours ticked by. In a matter of forty five minutes the four men were approaching the all so familiar cabin. Matt noticed Clifford's horse out front tied to the tie post. What he had planned, Matt had no idea. They pulled up next to Clifford's horse got down flipping the reins over the rail. Things seemed very quiet as they walked up the steps toward the front door. It was already cracked. Matt pushed it open and the men entered.

"Well, I didn't expect you so soon," Clifford started. "Who's your friends?" as he struck a match lighting a cigarette.

"These here are Tom and Trip," Matt answered.

"Where you two from?" Clifford asked, taking a drag from his cigarette and exhaling the smoke through his nose and mouth.

"Jackson Hole for the past six months running cattle," Tripp stated.

"You must have heard of Richard Goldman? He pushes more cattle through Jackson and any other rancher I know," Clifford asked.

"Yeah we know him, but we never drove for him," Matt answered.

"He had one hell of a beautiful daughter, Jill I think her name was. Real long golden hair," he stated. "If you knew Richard than you knew Jill."

"We met her but never was formally introduced," Tripp confessed.

"Of course. Because there is no Richard Goldman and there is no daughter Jill," Clifford retorted.

Knowing they had just been suckered they had two choices; go for their guns or try to bluff their way out.

Tripp tried to speak-up before Tom would go for his gun.

It was too late. Clifford had his gun out pointing at the two of them. Their chances of drawing and winning were gone.

"Richard Goldman is alive and well. Just as his daughter is," Clifford lied. "I had to test you to make sure you were who you said you were. You pass."

Tripp didn't know what to believe now. Was Clifford teasing or were they caught dead to rights?

When Clifford put his gun away they both let out a sigh of relief. A sigh that hopefully no one heard.

Matt and Steve also were in shock not knowing what had just happened. They listened letting Clifford do the talking. They would find out what the deal was later when they were alone with Clifford.

"Matt I don't want you or Steve to think I'm taking over. You can make the arrangements from here on out, but it will take the five of us to deliver the herd in a fair time frame to make it worth while. We need to be out of the territory with-in hours to avoid unwanted followers, if you know what I mean," Clifford surrendered.

Matt felt good when that was addressed to him and Steve. He just wanted to know more about Tripp and Tom. He thought for sure there would have been two dead bodies lying on the floor by this time.

"We best be getting back to town," Matt said. "Steve's horse has a loose shoe and we'll need to get it replaced before we start any long distance."

"Ok, you do that. We'll meet back here three hours after the rains start and get this job done," Matt ordered.

"Matt, you and Steve take the boys out back and grab some fire wood from the shed. I'll be staying here and I would like to have enough for the stove for dinner. Any one that would like to stay is welcome," Matt asked.

This seemed like a strange request to Matt but he somehow knew it was for a reason.

"Come on boys four of us ought to be able to make this in one load," he guessed.

The shed was about fifty feet away from the back porch. Each grabbed as much wood as they could and returned piling the wood on the back porch. Returning back-in Clifford was at the front door with the door wide open, looking out.

"Thanks fellas, get now and let's get the job done," he praised.

"When we get back to town you two get your horses taken care of and meet Steve and me in the saloon as quickly as possible," Matt ordered. "I'll take Tripp, Tom and Steve. We'll scout-out the ranches and see if we can find where the strays are located."

"Ok boss," Tom replied. "Let's get."

"Tonight we will head out. When the rain starts, we move in, round up as many as we can and get them out of the territory. Matt and Steve know where to bring them. I will-meet up with you some-where along the way and we will continue on," Clifford announced.

Riding back to town seemed long. There was no conversation between any of the men. Tripp was too deep in thought to talk anyway. What was Clifford up to? Was he the man he needed to be suspicious of?

The clouds were getting darker by the hour, Matt knew they would have to step up the operation to have it flow the way they designed it.

The town was quiet as they rode down Main Street. Matt and Steve stopped in front of the saloon.

"You and Tom go on ahead to the livery and get those horses looked at. Meet us back here when you're finished," Matt speaking up.

"See ya in a bit," Tripp answered.

Sucking up a few beers Tripp had a sudden need to walk down toward the livery and see how the boys were making out.

"I'll be back in a few," he announced downing what was left of his beer.

Two buildings down from the livery he was surprised to see Vince and Jeb stop at the livery. Being real curious of what he just saw, he slowly worked his way toward the livery, hoping to see or hear if there was any connection between the four men. His hunch was right. He was within fifty feet when he could see the four men in deep conversation. He watched for about ten minutes and then figured he had seen enough and slithered back to the saloon.

Steve was having small talk with the barkeep and one of the saloon girls.

"Steve!" He yelled, as he motioned him to come to a table where he pulled a chair. Your not gonna believe what I just saw. Tripp and Tom are down at the livery talking to Jeb and his friend."

"What you want to do?" Steve asked.

"Back at the ranch I noticed Clifford acting funny toward those two and when he sent us out to fetch the wood that two of us could have handled puzzled me too. Let's wait and tell Clifford what we saw and see what he wants to do," Matt said in question.

"Lets ride back out and tell Clifford," Steve recommended.

"No let's just see what they have to say when come in," Matt suggested. "See how nervous they seem."

Just as he had finished, the two came walking through the bat-wings just babbling on, laughing like nothing had happened.

"Got the shoes done already?" Matt asked as the two pulled a chair and sat.

"Not 'til morning," Tripp lied.

They sat around and drank, making small talk. Tripp started feeling uneasy but couldn't put his finger on any one thing.

"It's beginning to sprinkle," Tom reported. "I think I'm gonna get 'til tomorrow. I think it's gonna be a long day."

"I think so too," Matt stated.

CHAPTER 14

Vince and Jeb had left for the ranch after they spoke to Tripp and Tom.

"We're gonna have to get out early tomorrow brother," Vince said. "Those two are in a lot of danger and we put them there. If something happens to them it's gonna be on our heads. I have a bad feeling about this. If it continues to rain they're gonna be making their move sooner than planned. My bet is they'll use Tripp and Tom 'til they get the cattle delivered and then kill them. I don't think they intend to pay them one red cent. With lead probably."

"I know. Maybe we over-shot the boundaries but I think they can take care of themselves. I know where this cabin is. There's a big hill just to the West of it that will make for a good look out," Jeb replied. "We need to get with Ben and Barry. I put a couple of my best men on alert; Cliff and Johnny. They said they could be ready on a moments notice. We'll get Sam involved if and when we know something. I better get word to Ben and Barry tonight then. You get home to Jane and I'll ride out and circle to the two ranches. I should be home in a while."

"Ok but don't dally wag, I don't need to worry about you," Vince said as he spurred Colt and bolted for home.

"I'm a big boy," Vince heard coming from Jeb as he wheeled his horse around and galloped off.

Jeb returned home a few hours later with the news that everyone would meet at Brett's ranch in the early morning and then head out to keep an eye on the cattle.

"I volunteered us to go out to the cabin and keep a lookout on any activities that may start as the rain thickens," Jeb announced. "We need to catch them red-handed with the cattle to make any arrest stick."

"I think these men might be hard to arrest knowing that they're going to hang for the months of rustling they're responsible for," Vince responded. "I believe we'll be in for one hell of a shootout when they're confronted.

"Well, that's where I hope Tripp and Tom will come into play. Having them on the inside will be our ace in the hole. If Matt and Steve know anything about them then we could all be in a lot of danger," Jeb retorted.

As the night lingered the sound of rain was getting louder on the roof letting Jeb know they were going to have to get up at the break of dawn and move their rendezvous up with the others by a few hours.

Jane was feeling uneasy over what was happening but she knew that Vince's commitment with Jeb may be completed soon and everyone could relax and get back to life as normal. She knew how Jeb missed his brothers and hoped they would return when this was over. After all, he moved out here to be with them and now they moved on without him again.

Listening to the rain hit the roof was a relaxing sound and before long everyone was asleep. No hoot owls or coyotes would be heard this night.

Vince woke two times during the night to find Jane snuggled up to him drawing warmth from his body. Little Robert was at the foot of the bed in his rocking crib, wheezing the night way with dreams of what ever babies dream about. This made him think of how good everything was going in his life. He would have to enter into this fight with extreme caution to prevent anything from changing it.

He never did get back to a sound sleep except for minutes at a time. He was ready to get up and with luck get this over with today.

It wasn't long afterward when the knock he was expecting came gently on the door as not to wake Jane or the baby. He slipped out from under the covers throwing his clothes on and giving Jane and the baby a soft kiss on the cheek. He slipped out the door to meet Jeb who was waiting with hot mugs of coffee.

"Couldn't sleep any longer," he stated as he sipped hot coffee.

"I've been up for hours too," Vince admitted. "Just laying there thinking. I'll go saddle the horses. You throw some grub and coffee together."

He opened the door to find it still raining pretty hard with a chilly breeze that made him take deep exhilarating breaths.

"Dress warm Bud. I think it's gonna be a little cool 'til the rain calms down some," he warned Jeb.

They walked the horses away from the house so not to wake Jane or the baby and then mounted and put them to a gallop. Colt liked that but he wasn't as frisky because of the rain Vince thought. They made good time getting to the hill that over-looked the cabin. Horses were still in a make shift arena but there was movement out and around with smoke bellowing from the chimney. It wasn't long until they watched a couple of men walk out to the coral with bridals in their hands.

"We got here just in time, huh?" Vince questioned.

"Uh huh," Jeb responded.

It was less than a half hour before there were five men riding off. It was time now for Vince and Jeb to follow without being detected, yet not too far back to lose them. Everything was going to plan.

"Ok Vince, take off and get the others," Jeb ordered. I'll stay with them. It looks like they're heading toward Slocombs ranch."

"Be back in a flash," Vince returned as he reined Colt to a hard right.

Seconds later he was out of sight and the sound of Colts hooves faded into the falling rain. Jeb continued with caution to stay with the rustlers. He pulled his coat tight and adjusted the collar to make sure the rain water running off his hat wasn't going to find its way into his coat. The rain was falling pretty good. The horse tracks he was following were filling in almost totally making it harder to follow. He knew he had to close in some, knowing it was more of a dangerous move. He knew they were heading toward the ranch but they would be heading off in another direction to get the cattle they had probably bunched together at a near-by valley. He anticipated Vince and the others would catch up soon. It would be ten of his men against three and Tripp and Tom were two more he hoped he could count-on when the time came.

Twenty minutes later he saw the silhouettes of the others riding up behind him. He pulled back on the reins and waited. Once they were within a few yards, he reined his horse leading the pack in the direction of the rustlers.

The ground started to shake under their horses. They had the cattle and were herding them hard in the direction of their destination.

"Ok fellas. Lets close-in and get what we're after," Jeb ordered.

"Break off and come up on the sides but be careful of cross-fire if shooting starts. Be careful of Tripp and Tom."

Cliff and Johnny rode up on Steve who never noticed them until they were on top of him and it was too late. Johnny rode up tight and clubbed Steve to the side of his head knocking him to the ground and out of the fight. Ben and Charlie had beads on Matt before he knew they were on him and surprisingly surrendered knowing they had the drop on him. Clifford was herding cattle to the far right and caught sight of Jeb and Vince coming up on him. He had his gun pulled only to have it shot out of his hand by Vince. Tripp and Tom rode up glad to know a long and hard gunfight was avoided.

It was then the three knew that Tripp and Tom were decoys for the ranchers.

"What did I tell you," Clifford yelled. "I told you these two were no good."

"Remember how no good they are while you three are standing with ropes around your necks," Barry cautioned. "Ben, Charlie, you and the others get the herd back to the ranch. We'll sort them out later."

"Got it boss," Ben yelled. "Let's go boys. The sooner we get em back the sooner we can get back into dry clothes."

"Alright you three. You have a nice cozy jail cell waiting for you," Jeb retorted.

The three ranchers weren't about to lose these men so they all escorted them back to town and personally walked them into the jail. After everyone had left Jeb and Vince stayed to talk to the prisoners.

"How did you do this for so long without leaving any signs of a trail?" Jeb asked.

"We don't know," Matt was speaking for himself and Steve. "We were paid to bring them down to the valley and leave. We were told if anyone hung around they would be shot."

Vince looked over to Cifford, "Well how about it? If you weren't with these two then you must have been with the men that took them to the destination point."

Clifford just looked through Vince and Jeb. They knew they weren't gonna get anything from him.

"You're gonna hang for this. You might as well tell what you know. Why go down by yourself?" Vince asked.

Again Clifford just smiled with a blank stare.

"I'm gonna take a stab at how you did this. You tell me if I'm close," Vince started. "I did quite a bit of traveling around and I think I have more than a theory. I think that after these two with the rest of the men delivered the cattle to you and your clan where they were taken up the valley about twenty miles to the Arkansas River where you had cargo boats waiting. There you loaded them and took them down stream say about another twenty miles, where you then unloaded them and sold them to the Indians.

They took them to feed their people, skinning them and using the hides, thus leaving no trail for anyone to find."

Vince starred at Clifford and felt he was damn near right, he could see it in his eyes.

"Well how about it?" Vince asked again. "You might as well come clean, we're right and you know it. Shake your head if I'm right. What we want from you is to tell us who you worked for, who paid you for cattle you stole?"

Again Clifford clammed up but then Matt stood and walked over to the bars of the cell.

"You got something to say?" Jeb asked.

"We don't have a name. We worked for some guy by the name of Buster, but we never got a last name, just Buster. It was through him the orders came. We met the boss just once. It was when we were told to get out of town and never return. He promised our money but took off without paying us for our last job. Clifford either. We wanted to do this last job, get paid and were going to hunt him down and kill him," Matt confessed.

"Well now instead you're gonna pay with your lives. Did you ever hear the names Mike or Jake Ballard?" Vince asked.

"No," they agreed.

"Well Mike Ballard is the one who didn't pay you and took off with your money. This man you speak of, any idea where he went?" Vince asked with hope.

"If we did we'd sure tell you now, I'd like to see him just one more time. Get my hands around his cheating neck," Matt said angrily.

"Rest assured, if there's any chance at all, he'll be hanging right next to you three," Vince promised.

The territorial judge was to be in town in just days, so the men's fate wouldn't be drawn out. With all the evidence that was on them and their confession it was an open and shut case with only hanging being the only outcome.

CHAPTER 15

"We can't just sit here and do nothing," one man sitting at the card table mentioned to the other four. "We were just as much part of this as they were."

"Yeah, but we got out when we were told, nobody told them to go and rustle more cattle. As I remember it we were told to get out. Go back to our lives or get out of town never to return. Now you suggest we help these three?" Jack questioned.

"That's the only right thing to do. If they decide to stick around after we break them out then it's their heads," Fred responded.

"They know our names, they could squeal like pigs once that noose is around their necks. Do you want to take that chance? There's no sheriff assigned to the town, just the deputy, so it shouldn't be that hard," Jack assured them.

"Why don't we kill them like they did Tillman?" Fred asked.

"That's another option. Let's vote," Jack answered without thought, "But I think if we use our heads we can get them out pretty easy. Maybe without gun play."

"I've got it!" Fred yelled out, "We wait 'til the next time Jeb and his friend go to town. We pay his friend's wife a visit. Take them so a secluded place far enough away where they won't be found. Leave a note for an exchange for our men. When we know they're released we get rid of our witnesses and go back to our ranching like nothing has ever happened."

"I don't know about this, those two found out about the rustlers pretty fast," Jack said with concern. "Jebs friend is better than any blood hound I've ever seen. Sounds way too risky"

"You have a better idea let's hear it," Fred retorted, "It doesn't matter one way or another. Any of them boy's talk it's a rope around our neck and I don't feel much like being in that predicament."

Chapter 16

It was a hot afternoon, the hottest time of the day. Riding home Vince was doing a lot of thinking. Colt was dragging also as the heat took all the horse-play out of him. Vince let him have rein and went along for the ride as he kept a steady pace following the trail he had come to learn so well from all the trips he had taken to town.

As they turned the corner the ranch came into sight giving both relief. Colt knew he would get his normal rubdown, sack of oaks after some water and a pitch full of hay.

Every thing was relatively quiet. No dog was barking and most of the cats that found a home here at Jeb's place were scattered in different spots, some sleeping with others lying around licking, coughing up hair balls, but paying Vince no attention as he made ready to care for Colt before heading to the house.

Vince was anxious to get to the house to see Jane and little Robert. Hungry him self, he hurried to have that meal Jane usually had at his return.

Shutting the stall gate, Vince gave Colt a slap to his hind quarter and headed for the house.

Climbing the four steps to the porch he stopped for a few seconds to slap the trail dust off him-self not needing to bring it inside.

Opening the door he had no idea he would be walking into another big change in his life.

Entering the front door there were two explosions sending Vince backward and falling back off the front porch down into the dirt. Vince didn't move.

When his eyes opened again he had no idea how long he was out or where he even was. He found the room to be familiar but was in and out of conscious too fast to get bearings where he was. Each time he regained consciousness all he experience was excruciating pain. It hurt so bad he didn't want to try nor could he move a muscle. Breathing was very hard also but soon realized it was from a heavy wrapping around his full torso.

Going in and out of sleep now he would wake-up to feel the same pain.

Waking up he found it hard to focus. At first he thought Jane was at his bed side only to find Doc Adams as his eyes cleared and focused. Jeb walked in and stood next to Doc with looks of amazement.

Trying to speak he found nothing came out. He tried again only to have the doctor place his fingers over his lips and order him not to try.

"Where's Jane?" he managed to get out only to see Doc not respond. As if he didn't even hear.

Before he could try again he was out again.

Hours later his eyes opened and he struggled with the question once more.

"Where's Jane? Where's Robert?" he forced out in a loud whisper.

"Rest Vince," Doc responded.

"Answer me," he forced out this time to hear myself.

"We don't know Vince," Jeb retorted, "I rode-in to find you lying on the ground outside the door and found no one when I came in."

Vince tried so desperately to sit up but to no avail.

"Lie still," Doc yelled, "I can't do anything more for you if you open up those wounds again. You'll start to bleed inside and then you'll die. You should be dead already as it is."

"Vince, the sheriff and a pose are out looking for Jane as we speak. We found no one when we arrived, they may just have been kidnapped," Jeb said with sincerity.

Vince tried again to move to no avail. The pain was so bad. He found if he tried again he would pass out. For hours or minutes, he couldn't tell. Sleeping was the only comfort he witnessed. Dreaming Jane and Robert were there with him, he only woke to disappointment. He would find them by him self or with Jeb at his side.

Each time his eyes would open he found him-self more responsive and coherent than the time before.

What he thought were hours were actually days. He woke many times only to find Doc forcing some sort of liquid in his mouth which would put him out faster than he could realize. So fast that he couldn't remember how bad it tasted.

Now, each time he was waking he found the pain not so severe but did experience how bad the medicine tasted. Realizing this must be making him heal he stopped fighting, and let his body take over.

Each time he woke things became clearer. The drug Laudanum was a drug to kill the massive pain and make him sleep, but it was the hallucinating that gave him a time. Realizing this, he cut back on his dosage so he could start thinking straight. Doc did his job well and further reduced the dosages as he saw improvement in his patient.

It was two weeks now. Time was making him more coherent of what happened.

"Jane and Robert,' he kept calling.

"They're still looking for them, Vince," Jeb promised.

"Where are they? Where are they? Who, who has them?" he kept asking.

Jeb and Doc thought it was time to let Vince know what they knew.

"You walked into an ambush Vince," Jeb started. "The men responsible came in from the back of the house and caught Jane off guard. They left a note demanding the release of the horse thieves in exchange for the safe return of Jane and the kid."

"What's the Sheriff going to do?" he asked.

"The men were hung two days ago, Vince," Doc confessed.

"Vince, I'm sorry to tell you this but four days ago a wagon rolled into Sunny Valley a small town from here. Jane and Robert's bodies were in the back. The doc in town thinks they were poisoned," Jeb surrendered.

Suddenly it was as if I was shot in the stomach. I wasn't but the pain was just as excruciating.

Doc put a cup to my mouth and ordered me to take a sip. I don't remember him pulling the cup away before I fell back into the sleep I had been experiencing.

When I woke a day later Doc explained it was necessary to continue to keep me under to keep myself from hurting myself or worse. At this point I found my heart so empty that I wish he had let me go.

"When will I be able to get up?" I asked the doc.

"I'd say in about a week if you stay still," he announced. "Those bullets both came close to being victorious in taking your life. There's no infection but your body needs to heal inside as well as out. There's nothing more I can do so it's up to you how fast you recover and its rest you need to accomplish that."

I was just too tired to argue so I let my body go limp and tried to relax.

CHAPTER 17

Every day became a new challenge. He was now getting to the point of sitting up. Doc was changing bandages regularly but still keeping the wrap tight. He then started having him try to sit, stand and take steps. There was nothing wrong with his legs or arms but the pains in his upper body were still devastating.

Doc left a bottle of pain reliever knowing that it wouldn't be abused.

In this pain and slow recovery he continuously thought of chugging it down and ending this miserable life. Something always brought him coherent enough to hold back that thought. In his dream sleep, Jane would tell him to go on. Or it was the pain killer that helped him recover quickly.

Jeb had been letting Colt and Star out in the coral where they could stretch and roam somewhat free. Colt bucked and ran wildly, sensing something had happened to me.

Forcing him out to the porch one day where Colt could see him settled him down to stare 'til he returned back to bed. Seeing Star was different. His heart dropped knowing Jane would never be riding him again or that Robert wouldn't be here to have riding lessons.

Who in the world could experience losing two families in one life time? Vince's life was resurrected when he met Jane and then they were blessed with Robert. It helped him cope with the loss of his family and now both of them were gone. Thinking of revenge for the men who were responsible already entered his mind yet something held his thoughts back from going off the deep end. Get better first he kept telling him self.

Jeb was always near to help keep a positive attitude. Vince was to the point of getting out side and stretching his healing body. He would push myself to the point to where he couldn't stand the pain any longer, then return back to the house.

Two more weeks had gone by when he decided the need to get on a horse. Colt couldn't be ridden in his condition so Jeb saddled Star and rode out letting Colt follow. What started out to be a short ride lasted a couple of hours. The clear and warm weather was healing. It did the body good. The country-side was so relaxing he thought only positive thoughts and took-in all the freshness his body could stand. Returning, one of Jeb's hands were there to take the horses back to the stable.

Jeb tried to convince his friend to stay-on to help him with the ranch and was even offered the job as Sheriff which both he had to gracefully decline. Knowing there had to be a place in this country where he would find his destiny.

Visiting the resting place of Jane and Robert daily, he often hoped for a sign to know where he should start his life over again.

CHAPTER 18

Waking up one morning Vince felt different. He knew he was now a changed man. So mad at what life handed him, he made himself a promise. One that no normal man would ever make. He was out for revenge for anyone who would put any innocent man, woman or child in danger. He vowed to protect anyone and do so with no interest of wearing a badge, just the tool he was accustomed to.

No mention would be made of this to anyone. Not even Jeb.

It had been months since the shooting took place and he was feeling ready to pack and leave. Where, he had no idea. If he decided to return back to his dad's ranch it would be the long way. Knowing every town had bad men hanging around taking advantage of the weak held his interest. Jeb was really puzzled when Vince out of the blue made the announcement he was leaving by the end of the week. Yet it came as no surprise.

Star would have to stay behind. Giving the horse to Jeb along with saddle and bridle was a small gift of friendship. Always fancying Jane's saddle and bridle, he wanted it to be with him just as having wanting her along. In his mind she would be.

Seeing how good Colt looked with the black studded saddle and bridal it really gave him a good feeling.

Saying goodbye to such a great friend was hard but it was done and he left with his hands cupping the saddle horn and headed Colt toward his destiny. There was no going into town for any good byes.

It was the second day on the trail when he finally decided to find a camp site off the path to spend the night. Finding a place where he could practice with his gun and know where shots would be muffled by thick trees and bushes. Having plenty of ammunition he planned to use as much as it took to sharpen his skills back to where they had always been. With his new life he knew he would have to be on top of his game to survive and he planned on living long and hard.

Finding the place to bed down that was heavily covered with trees and bushes. Green as green could be. A man could choose to build a ranch and live out his days in such beautiful country. The birds were in harmony as well as crickets and frogs. Places like this would be restful he knew deep inside a place like this was just perfect. He already dreaded leaving it in such a short time. Pulling the saddle from Colt and brushing him down was no chore at all. Colt was already enjoying the green grass that was long and plentiful. The camp fire would have to wait as he headed deep into the woods to do some shooting. With just a few pulls of his pistols he found the speed was still remarkably fast but he spent many cartridges making sure. He knew a splint second could mean life or death, so some extra practice wasn't an option in his my mind.

The fire was bright and warm and the beef stew and biscuits really hit the spot. Later that evening he found himself staring into the fire relaxing and letting his mind wander. Sliding the saddle to the back of his head he was instantly falling into a long hard sleep.

Morning came fast but waking he remembered the great dreams he had encountered that night with Jane and Robert taking up his time on the most wonderful ranch one could imagine. Vince soon found that his night dreams would be better than reality and looked forward to sleeping to encounter more.

The fire was still smoldering but answered the call as he threw some small twigs on to enhance it. Pulling some bacon, biscuits and coffee, breakfast was ready in a flash and wasn't half bad. Colt enjoyed a few handfuls of oats and showed his approval with some head-shaking snorting.

Leaving this place and moving out was hard to do but it was in his interest to find the next town which was probably a few days away. The Indians could come between them, which was a concern. He had no feud with them, and hoped they had none for him.

Miles out, the mountain ranges on two sides were red as could be with little green interfering with it's stillness. Staying alert and watching for any movement that may catch an eye. Colt had great perception of danger and was exceptional in perking his ears to alert immediate danger. His hooves striking the surface of the trail was all Vince could hear. Colt had to be as bored as Vince as time went on. Suddenly Colt slammed to a halt. All boredom came to a halt. Vince, half in a trance, was damned near thrown over his head by Colt stopping so quickly.

Listening and squinting his eyes, he panned the area, carefully taking time covering every nook and cranny on both sides of the mountains, checking for any movement or ambush site, but saw nothing.

Even though it took only seconds, it felt like eternity. Wham! A bullet hit the ground about twenty yards in front of him followed by the thunder of the shot. Observing that, he knew they were safe for the moment. If they continued going it would put Colt in danger, but for the moment they were out of range. It took a few moments to decide what to do. Putting Colt in danger he would not chance.

He was too big a target and Vince would rather take another bullet than he. Dismounting and knowing a whistle would bring Colt running, he grabbed his rifle, turned Colt and slapped him to send him back in the direction they had just came. Standing very still, he listened for any warning. It was so still he swore he could hear lizards slithering along the desert sands.

Then it happened, the intimidating yells of Indians riding hard toward him. Shots came before the bullets hitting the dirt all around. Vince knew he was relatively safe as long as they were shooting while riding, so he was in no hurry to return fire. Seeing the dust trail heading his way, seconds were clicking off as the dust gave way to the silhouettes of five riders riding wildly toward him. This was to his advantage as they were slightly spread out. Shooting a horse was something Vince didn't want to do, but if they got on him too fast he knew he wouldn't have a chance. So he decided if he needed to shoot horses in order to slow them down he would have no choice.

Lifting his rife he carefully took aim. Squeezing off his first shot he watched the first of the assailants fall back off his horse. Levering his rifle he kept himself from panicking, took careful aim and squeezed the trigger ever so carefully. After the thunder from the rifle the second victim fell off to the side of his horse. It was then a bullet whistled by his head. Three more killers to shoot with only seconds left before they were on him. Levering the rifle again, taking aim and again watching the third fall back. He could see the fight was leaving the last two as he levered the rifle again. He had to get both even if they turned to retreat. If either could get away he'd have a tribe on him before he could get to the next town. The fourth hit the ground and the fifth turned to run. He was close enough that Vince knew to take his time and make the shot true. Seeing him fall to the ground he took a sigh of relief and stood there a moment to regain his composure.

Turning he gave a big whistle and watched as Colt came running. He mounted and sat there looking, watching, and waiting for any movement. The bodies of each assassin laid still. Cautiously he approached the five to make sure each was dead. They were out to kill and rob. The worst part was, they would have scalped him and carried his hair off for their trophy. Knowing this was quite bothersome. As much as he wanted to circle around and get traveling, he felt he had a responsibility. Riding up he saw they were Sioux. Approaching each of them with gun drawn he could see all but one had been carrying a new Winchester. Someone has been selling guns to the Indians and that was a hanging offense.

He knew not to bury these five knowing their own people would find and take them back for their own final send-off. Tying the rifles to his bed roll, he climbed back on Colt and continued on his way. It would now be his responsibility to find who sold these rifles to the Indians and take care of them accordingly. There was a time he cared about human life, but as he looked at it now, he was almost killed. The way he saw it, the men selling these rifles were responsible for this experience. One thing good that came from this, he came out unscathed and the monotony of these days of riding was broken. At least for now.

Figuring it was no more than two days out from the next town, he thought of how a good hot bath would help his weary sore bones and muscles. Sleeping on the ground catches up after a time, leaving the body yearning for a nice soft bed to sink into.

Vince watched along the mountains, on each side, staying as alert as possible. The day had been long and hot with few clouds to block the sun for even a few minutes. He began scouting ahead for some brush, bushes or inlet for a safe campsite. He was tired and sore and even Colt was beginning to slow from the heat. Vince knew they were approaching civilization as he began to see multiple tracks all around from either hunters or ranchers out looking for strays.

Finally a patch of green was spotted off to the left. It was made-up of dark green bushes and full branched trees showing plenty of protection and by the health of the growth he was sure the area was sitting on top of a large spring. This meant cold fresh water for himself and Colt. Hopefully this would be a place for a long relaxing bath before they headed into any town. Finding twigs and branches was easy. Apparently this place was not visited as much as he would have guessed. It worried him at first because he didn't need to be awakened by a knife to his throat or a gun pressed against his head. Colt was quiet and was his security alarm, but as tired as they both were, he felt he may not be as alert as normal.

The fire took quite fast and he had a slab of beef sizzling in a pan with coffee brewing in no time. He wiped-down

Colt and threw a blanket over him for the night. Leaving him short reined so he could turn his head or pull it off if he wished. Finishing the meal, he found himself a bit full eating a few more biscuits than usual.

The harmony of frogs and crickets broke the silence as the evening wore on. The stars were out and the moon was at its fullest. A good time to wonder down to the stream to wash off all the saddle dust his body sucked up from riding the plains. His skin shrunk to his body as he entered the cold running water of the brook. A nice deep pool swallowed his body making it easy to wash both his body and hair. In less than an hour he was bedding down, knowing he was in for a good nights sleep. Pulling the covers tight he made sure his pistol was readily assessable. Not even remembering falling asleep he fell into dream world. Waking a few times during the night Vince laid there thinking of what he might be riding into when he rode into the next town. He didn't favor traveling by himself. He was used to traveling with a partner and friend, then with a new wife and best friend who he was supposed to finish his life with.

He must have fallen back to sleep because he was startled awake by the sound of a broken branch. Grabbing his pistol he laid still, letting his eyes focus to the early morning light. The face as just too familiar, big black eyes, a face that was just inches away. Telling him to get up, that he over slept. He reached up and slapped him one on the nose.

"Ok, boy. You win. I'm up," he teased.

The fire from last night was hot enough to fire up the small branches thrown into the ashes. Presto, he now had a small camp fire to heat up some coffee and biscuits. Colt had found some nice green grass at the edge of the stream to satisfy his hunger and thirst. Sitting around awhile when he finished, he felt well rested and ready to finish the next leg of the ride hoping that the next town was no more than one days ride. Having a weakness for such restful places like this it was always hard to leave. Knowing he wasn't in any hurry, he sat back and wasted a few hours before getting back on the trail.

It was mid afternoon as they rode over a rise that he spotted a small town just miles away. Soon a sign proclaimed "Welcome to San Miguel," population three hundred. A cold beer was already being anticipated. Thinking it would be nice to sit with the company of a soft spoken young lady after such a long ride.

Not being in any hurry and wanting some time to study the surroundings he let Colt have the reins and stroll at his own pace. Vince had an uneasy felling right away.

There were no kids running around. Very few women were walking the streets. No one seemed to be in any hurry, but out of the corner of his eyes he could see he was being studied by some of the men they rode past. It was the two men he caught a glimpse of who scurried into the saloon. Off to the immediate left was the sheriff's office, it was there he would visit first. Flipping Colts reins over the tying post he stepped up onto the walk-way and entered. There sat a white haired man who looked more stressed than old. A quick glimpse suggested the office looked bigger inside than on the outside. One wall had a gun rack providing a resting place for two double barrel shotguns and three 44-40 Winchesters. At a closer look he could see they were older rifles.

"What can I do for you friend?" the sheriff said as he looked up.

The look on his face assured Vince he was giving him a good close once over.

"Came to talk to you about some trouble I had about forty miles west," he answered. "Indians, Sioux, they came to me on at fast pace and it wasn't to smoke no peace pipe. I ended killing five of them. They were all welcoming me with lead from their brand new Winchesters. At least four of them were."

"Forty miles out huh?" he questioned. "We haven't had any trouble with Indians for some time now. This was self defense I presume?"

"You presume right," as he went on to tell him what actually happened.

He sat in silence and studying my story for some time before Vince broke the silence.

"I have the rifles wrapped in my bed roll outside on my horse," he surrendered.

They walked outside to Colt and again Vince saw him studying the reins and saddle.

"You're either well off or maybe a lucky poker player?" he guessed.

"Let's just keep focused on what's in my bed roll, can we?" Vince retorted.

"Bring them inside and we'll take a look," he asked, even though he saw him already untying the bedroll.

They both went back inside where Vince laid the roll on a table and unwrapped some of the most outstanding rifles.

"New alright," the sheriff admitted. "I wouldn't mind having one of these my self."

"So, you're surprised to see such guns carried by Indians?" Vince asked. "No word-out that gun running has been a problem in the area?"

"Not exactly friend," he answered. "But this is the first actual evidence I've seen."

"This is the closest town in range of Indians," Vince stated. "If they are interested in an uprising, this place is a sitting duck. How close is the nearest town?"

"Let's just say that if we were attacked or we even thought we would be attacked, no one could get help here in time." The sheriff conceded.

Vince looked into space thinking. He didn't need to be in any part problem with Indians. He had already decided what his intentions were. No way was he going to be detoured.

"How long you figuring on staying in town," the sheriff asked Vince.

"Don't rightly know, but wasn't intending on a long stay," he answered. "I'm going to get me a drink and a hot meal. Join me?"

"Maybe in a while. I want to ponder on what this could all mean. I think I'll telegraph Durango and see what I can find out," the sheriff responded.

"See you there," Vince remarked as he turned heal and went out the door.

The evening was cool. Looking to the sky there wasn't a clue of any rain in sight. The nice cool breeze was welcome. Heading for the hotel, Vince figured on getting a room and hot bath before heading back down to dinner. This would give the sheriff time to finish his pondering. He planned to stay no more than a day, then head south for Albuquerque.

The hot water immediately went to work on sore weary bones and tense muscles as Vince settled in. He laid his head back and laid there enjoying the relaxation he missed. Soon after he noticed the abuse his body had taken in the past year. The pain seemed to be constant, but realized he was lucky to be alive. Feeling alone, he knew he had no one to turn to if he got into a jam and would have to prove his innocence. Wanting to hit the sack and call it a night, getting some food was a priority. Food that men ate out in the range did not give the body ultimate values. It was quite a ride to Albuquerque. Getting back into shape in any from was not an option.

Heading down stairs it seemed to be on the quiet side. Entering the dinner he could see the sheriff had already seated himself and was waiting for his company.

"Well the bath did you some good. You look quite refreshed," the sheriff commented.

"Yes, yes it did, thank you," Vince courteously responded. "It was hard to get myself down here. I was ready to lay down a spell, but I knew that would have been it if I did."

"I received a response from the telegram I sent with your information, and already received one back saying there's a brigade already on the way and should be in the area within days. So I guess you were right. I guess thanks are in order," the sheriff remarked. I guess the least I can do is buy your dinner.

"It's not necessary, sheriff, but appreciated," Vince responded.

After dinner Vince was refreshed and thought he might check and see if he might get into a poker game to test his luck.

Stepping up to the bar he ordered a beer and fanned the tables looking to see if there might be a table he would fit-in with. Off to the right there was a man leaving a table which left a vacant seat but it would place his back to the bat wings. He didn't fancy that so he turned, ordered another drink and patiently waited. It was getting late in the evening and he knew there would be an open seat shortly. As luck would have it one can up a few minutes later. Walking over, he asked if he could join-in and was motioned to sit down and ante-up. Reaching into his pockets he pulled out only a few bills and laid them on the table. The game commenced. Only four were at the table including him. Feeling his odds were good, the men seemed hospitable so he relaxed and sat back to enjoy an hour or so of stud poker, win or lose.

It lasted about an hour when he felt he was up just enough to call it quits. He stood up stretching his muscles and as he did so he caught the eye of a man at the bar that seemed to nod him to come over. Cautiously he walked over and saw a beer had already been poured for him by the gentleman.

"What can I do for you friend?" Vince asked in a quiet voice.

"It's not what you can do for me, it's what I can do for you," the man returned.

There was a man in here a couple of days ago asking about a man who rode a horse just like the one you rode in here with. I told him no, but that was because I hadn't. Then when I saw you ride-in this afternoon it rang a bell."

"That man still in town?" Vince asked.

"No. He said he was heading east. Said he had family there and said he was a friend of yours, but I'm a pretty good judge of character and I think he was looking for you for another reason and the men accompanying him were for sure hired guns. I didn't know them and I don't know you. I usually mind my business and stay out of trouble, but I see now you're on your own and heading for some possible trouble. Fair is fair so I felt obligated to tell you."

"Well maybe this was the best hand of the night," Vince answered. "Thanks for the information and I'll watch out- even though I don't know of anyone who would be looking for me."

It wasn't until he was walking out when everything this man just told him rang a bell. Why didn't this register while the man was speaking? It had to be Mike Ballard. He knew Mike couldn't out-shoot or beat him in a fair fist-fight, so that's why the hired men. He felt his innards start to churn with anger. So much that it would be hard to hold-in.

CHAPTER 19

"How could a man riding such a fancy horse and saddle not be noticed?" Mike Ballard asked his two associates. "This isn't a ghost we're looking for. Someone has had to see him."

"How do you know he's heading east? Maybe he went west or south. Why are you so sure he's come this way?" Johnny asked.

"Because I know!" Mike yelled with annoyance.

"Why are you so anxious to find this man when we passed on his friend Jeb?" Johnny asked again.

"Because we are the lucky ones who got out of the area with our necks still in place," Mike answered. "Bet they're still looking for anyone connected with that whole operation. There are still men taking their chances staying and if they get caught you wouldn't want to bet your life they wouldn't talk now, would you?" Mike retorted. "Jebs time will come at a future time, ok?"

"Makes sense except I'm not sure I want to return, not for any reason," Johnny returned.

"You'll do as you're told or you'll be dead," Mike promised. "You have any problem understanding that, John?"

"No Mike, I guess not," Johnny answered knowing Mike had influence over his men.

"The way I figure it, maybe he's behind us, not ahead. So we can continue on and see no one or hold up a few days and see what happens," Mike guessed aloud.

Meanwhile Johnny was working on a scheme to take Mike out before he was eliminated himself. If it didn't happen soon it was a sure thing it would happen down the road. Johnny knew that once doubt was put in Mike's head about someone it never left. He knew he had just done that. He could try to shoot it out here. Knowing he could get Bonner. Maybe he'd plug Buster. Heck maybe all three as good as he was. But he knew it was a sure thing he would be shot in the process and he didn't favor that chance at all. He could wait 'til night and ride-out while the others were sleeping. He knew they wouldn't come after him, not as bad as Mike wanted his brother's killer, but guessed he would have to face one of them in the future. Yes, that's what he would do. He would head for Albuquerque. That was south of Mike's destination. Yeah, that's what he decided.

The sky looked clear with only spots of clouds. The moon was already in full view and even though it wasn't full it looked as if it would give enough light to ride by. Johnny took it real easy to save as much energy as he could. The others were enjoying their whisky and beer. Needing to stay sober and alert he made each beer last in a way no one would notice. He planned on getting himself a lot of distance before he started feeling safe. He also planned on heading-out in one direction, doubling back a few different times to throw off anyone who may be interested.

Johnny liked Bonner and Buster. He was sure to miss them after he left. He wished he could trust them enough to join-up, but that was too big of a chance to take. He mentally inventoried what he had in his saddle bags for traveling. He would need ammunition. He had enough clothing and blankets to stay warm. Food he knew he could get when needed as he was a crack shot with his pistol or rifle. Water holes seem to be plentiful. He just had to wait until the others went to sleep and quietly slip out.

The camp fire still had a small flame and was popping or crackling in no special rhythm. The moon was higher now and snoring assured him the others were asleep. One thing of caution is that sleeping on the range was different than a comfortable bed in a hotel. Men slept light in bed rolls with saddles as pillows. So when he started his departure, he would have to take it slow and easy.

The moon was straight overhead. Johnny had spent hours watching it. It was time to make his move. He had loaded his saddle bags, bed roll and saddle already. Just three things he needed to carry off in one trip to his horse. Slowly he slipped the saddle bags over his left shoulder, laid the bed roll over the saddle and placed it on his bent left arm to cradle it. He then lifted his rifle with his right arm where it could be aimed and fired in a second. Slowly he headed to the horses tied behind bushes which helped him sneak his way. Once there, he untied all the horses, threw the saddle over his and quietly and slowly led them off. The others followed. Once a hundred yards away, he saddled his horse as quickly as possible, mounted and headed out. Not watching or caring, the other three horses eventually went their own way.

Johnny was now safely on his way. All he had to do was double back a few times, ride on hard ground and in water as much as he could to hide his tracks. He felt a relief of having his freedom back, not having to take orders or be threatened by a mad man.

He didn't know how long it would take to get to Albuquerque but by mid morning he knew he would be far enough away to not care. The sound of each step his horse took

Registered in Johnny's ears and he found himself counting the steps, at times, just to keep from tiring. Every strange sound he heard found his hand dropping to the handle grip of his pistol.

Morning was chilly and clammy. As the men woke they were ready for a full mug of hot coffee. When they realized Johnny was missing, the thought of coffee was forgotten.

"I'll kill him," was the first words spoken, and it was Mike who spoke them.

The other two sat there dumb-founded for a few minutes, not knowing what to say. They knew Mike wouldn't kill. It would be one of them that would do that task and that didn't set well with either one of them. They too were about fed up with Mike giving orders, but the money was too good to deny. Actually they were envious of Johnny for having the guts to leave.

Finally Bonner got the fire going from the hot coals from the night before and started boiling the water for coffee. Then he sat back and rolled a cigarette. Buster was ripping off a piece of beef jerky with teeth like a Neanderthal, not waiting for the biscuits and bacon. Mike sat there watching both, steaming inside, with anger of what Johnny did. How dare he defy the man who considered himself the boss? How men thought of themselves who had power and money.

"So what do you have to say about this?" Mike snapped breaking the silence.

The two looked at each other and both knew they needed to choose their words carefully. Mike was fast becoming a loose cannon and that made him a dangerous man.

He had the influence to turn men on each other and both Bonner and Buster knew that.

"What should we think, boss? Buster finally answered.

"He seemed to be the odd one of the three of us," Bonner responded. "Always keeping to himself, never shared his thinking with nobody. Not even Buster or me. What are you thinking?"

"I want him dead," Mike answered.

Bonner thought to himself how Mike's hit-list was growing. How much longer would it be before he and Buster were on that same list?

Neither man had it in them to confide with each other with the question concerning the situation they were in. Each worried that one would warn Mike and the other would find himself dead. So they kept shut.

"Let's worry about the job at hand," Mike announced. "We'll take one job at a time."

"Whatever you say boss," Bonner said, looking over to Buster to check his expression.

Buster was expressionless.

The rest of the morning was spent with small talk. The three sat there eating their breakfast in near total silence, starring at anything but each other. Each man wondering what the other was thinking.

Chapter 20

Vince was eager to head out after Mike Ballard but if it were true Ballard was heading east, he could wait. He knew he would catch up with him at a later time. He had already made his plans for the route back home and he would stick to it.

He woke refreshed and alert. Sleeping-in an extra hour was something he needed. The next leg of his journey would be long, his body still healing. He took his time washing up and getting dressed. He went down stairs for a good hot breakfast, filling up on as much as his belly would hold. This would be the last good wholesome meal for a long time. The place was quiet with only a few patrons sitting scattered around the room. There was no pretty gal like Jamie waiting on customers. When he was done he sat back and enjoyed his fourth cup of coffee. His next stop was the general store for supplies then he would head for the stable. Realizing the long miles ahead didn't rightly delight him.

Walking to the store he noticed the streets were no busier than the day he rode in. The stable seemed pretty bare but Colt looked refreshed and Vince noticed his ears perk up when he came into view. Grabbing a handful of oats he treated his horse before he saddled up.

The sheriff was standing outside his door as Vince rode by. Nothing was said. Vince tipped his head and continued by.

"Good luck my friend," the sheriff said under his breath.

Vince was thinking the same thing for the sheriff and the whole town, hoping the cavalry arrived before the Indians did.

Vince had no special plans. He had no idea of what he was going to do. He wanted to be left alone and travel, with no definite plans, no schedule. He would ride and travel to his destinations with time of no importance. His next town was Albuquerque and he would not be diverted. He would travel and ride the many towns on his path home, looking and listening for clues or names of men who could be connected with Jane's and Roberts death. Then avenge them accordingly.

When he was satisfied he had found all his family's killers he would return home to decide if he fit the life style awaiting him.

It was a four to five day ride to Albuquerque which was all desert. Any water found along the way he would have Colt fill his belly and make sure all canteens were full. He looked to the sky and saw it was going to be a hot trip all the way. If it got too hot he would travel late at night and through the mornings when the weather was the coolest.

It was his second day on the trail coming to a rise when he heard gun fire. Spurring Colt he darted toward the bellows of rifle fire. Rising to the top of the next rise he was looking down to see a wagon leaving quite a tail of dust. Further back he saw five horses leaving their own dust trail pursuing the wagon. Figuring he would intercept the wagon about the same time the pursuers could close, he spurred Colt and began to close in on the triangle. He pulled his rifle and fired a shot into the air to let the pursuers know help was on the way. He hoped when they saw him coming they might retreat, but that didn't happen. He only had one choice now and that was to pursue the pursuers. When he was a hundred yards out he pulled the reins back hard bringing Colt to a quick halt. Then he again pulled his Winchester from the sheath, took careful aim and squeezed off a shot. Seconds after the rifle bellowed he saw a rider roll off the back of his horse and hit the ground. The second rider fell back, but it was from a shot from the wagon. He took aim and fired again. This time the man fell off the horse catching his boot in the stirrup and was dragged off the east yelling and dying slowly. The other two now saw it was foolish and retreated. The wagon came to a stop as Vince approached.

"Don't know who you are mister, but thanks, you just saved our hides," the driver yelled.

Vince saw the man riding shotgun was hit in the leg and in grimacing in pain.

"Let's look at that leg mister. You got a two days ride to the next town. You'll bleed to death if we don't stop that bleeding," he warned. "Why were they after you?"

"Don't rightly know, supplies maybe? We've been on the trail for days now. Maybe they thought we were easy prey for cargo. Take us out then sell the cargo in the next town. They would have done pretty good too. Men do the darnedest things for a buck," the driver said. "Supplies are at a premium out here in the smaller towns. We been doing pretty good delivering goods out here," the driver bragged.

"Rocky's the name," he introduced. "This here is Matt."

"Vince," he nodded to the two men.

"Have a last name, Vince?" Rocky asked.

"No," Vince answered convincingly. "Surprised you haven't run into any soldiers," quickly changing the subject.

"Seen no one for days," Rocky stated. "Soldiers? What in heavens for?"

"Sioux are on the war path and the town you're heading to is no match for a uprising," Vince answered. "They're heavily armed with Winchesters that someone's been selling them."

"Gun runners, huh? I can see where that could be a problem," Matt said.

After wrapping Matt's leg to the best of his ability Vince said his good bye, mounted Colt and continued on his way, wishing the two men their best. He stopped and turned, watching them ride on until they were out of sight.

He stopped to see if he could find any identification on the dead men lying on the trail. Going through their pockets he stripped all the pockets of any paper and money.

He stood there examining everything from each body. Putting everything in a sack he packed them in his saddle bags figuring he'd let the sheriff of the next town take care of it. He left the bodies knowing their buddies would be back to take care of them. Knowing, when they find out he took all the identification, they would for sure decide to come after him. Vince knew they were out there hiding and watching to see who checked on the bodies. Not caring and almost daring them he took his time and slowly rode on his way giving them, plenty of time to catch up to him.

He had plenty of time since it would take the others time to bury their three friends. Later finding a place to set up camp, he would find time to clean his rifle and have it ready if and when needed.

Helping people was Vince's destiny now. He felt pretty good how his life had now re-started. He could find no remorse for the three men he left back on the trail and knew there were plenty more just like them who chose to take the easy way, taking what others worked so hard to get.

His way of thinking may not sit well with the law, but he knew it was truly appreciated by the weaker or unsuspecting families who were struggling along to exist out here in the west.

Vince never looked for trouble but now he would put himself in the middle of anything that could get an outlaw looking to prey off some poor sole by tricking them or strong-arming them for their money or possessions.

Off in the distance he saw the dust of many horses. This had to be the cavalry heading north. They had to be better than three miles away. Not wanting to loose any more time he directed his path in a way to pass leaving at least a mile between them.

They should catch up to Rocky's wagon with-in a few hours, giving them safe passage for the rest of their journey.

When Vince knew the cavalry was behind him, he found himself thinking again of where he was bound for. He really like this country and wasn't sure he was doing right by leaving it. Knowing he could return at any time made him feel a whole lot better. He missed Jeb and yearned for his wife and son but snapped back realizing it wasn't to be.

Rounding the bend of some thick woods he found the perfect place to bed down for the night. The evenings were always outstanding. If the clouds were absent, the sunsets were like paintings he remembered seeing at the finer hotels he had visited. He found himself watching the sun disappear behind the horizon. He would stare for minutes making sure he saw the whole thing vanish, then enjoyed the painted sky it left behind.

He felt tired and knew a good night's sleep would charge his body enough to help travel many more miles tomorrow. He quickly tended to Colt, laid out his bed roll, started a small fire to detour varmints and within minutes was bedded down, sound asleep. No food or drink tonight. He was just too tired, too exhausted.

It was near four hours into the night when he was startled awake suddenly by the sound of breaking limbs. The fire he had started was gone and it was pitch dark. Not even enough moon light to help him adjust his eyes. He laid there with his gun in hand, listening. Colt was not stirring and that puzzled Vince. He then noticed the breeze was blowing down-wind from Colt, answered why he didn't alert him. Could it be a coyote or possibly one of the surviving men from back at the wagon? He laid there froze, refusing to let a muscle move. There was no growl, so that eliminated a coyote.

Minutes seemed like hours. He stayed low hoping that if whatever it was would come close enough he would be able to see a silhouette in the horizon giving him the advantage if he needed to shoot.

Just as he was getting frustrated and ready to make a move the wind changed. Colt was down wind of the breeze and caught the sent immediately. Giving a snort and shuffling his hooves there was an astounding reaction and Vince about came out of his skin as he saw an enormous mass jump directly over him. He could feel his heart jump to his throat and there wasn't even a chance to squeeze off a shot. The sound of thundering hooves disappeared into the darkness.

It was about the biggest buck Vince had ever seen. He laid there, his heart pounding as if to escape through his chest. Colt was already calmed, but Vince was now realizing that if that were a bear or mountain lion he would have been torn to pieces.

Lying there thinking and wondering he eventually nodded back off to sleep.

Morning came fast and Vince immediately let his mind take him back to last night. Looking over to the camp fire he realized he should have put a few larger logs on. It wasn't even smoldering. Thinking how tired he was and how by not taking the time to make a fire that would smolder through the night it could have cost him his life.

Getting up he started a new fire for coffee while he collected his composure.

This was one morning he was looking forward to get back on the trail and reach the next town where he could feel safe and clear his mind of all that happened. This was something that never affected him so. Hopefully it never would again.

Gathering and packing his gear he was in for another long hot day. Looking at his map he could see he was heading for Santa Fe Territory and the next big town in the journey was Santos Domingo. Looked like a long ride. He was already hoping he would run into a small town somewhere in-between. He momentarily forgot about distance as Jane and Robert entered his mind. Sleeping did his body good only to wake and have his insides knot up from what he had been through. He wanted vengeance and it didn't necessarily have to come to the men who were directly connected to his problem. He would clear a path for many good people who were affected by bad men and unable to fend for themselves. Finding the law was not effective enough in many cases, he would gladly take up the slack to help the needy.

When he got to Santos Domingo he would telegram Jeb as promised and wait for a response before moving on.

Vince was finding the trail he was traveling was not one heavily used.

Seeing the cavalry passing through days earlier, he was sure they helped pave the way for safe traveling.

The morning was uneventful and watching the same scenery for miles was becoming quite boring. Hours into the ride he decided to stop and stretch. It must have been early afternoon. He finished giving Colt a handful of oats, and was finishing the last piece of jerky, when he heard the pounding of horse hooves. There were three, he figured, all traveling at a fairly good pace. Thinking that it was unusual for riders to push their horse's so hard in such warm weather.

As they came into sight, Vince stood next to Colt and watched as the riders approached.

The men pulled back on the reins of their mounts as Vince caught their vision and they came closer at a slow gallop then to a slow paced walk.

Vince could see these three were pretty rough looking hombres, so he immediately went into defense mode until he could find out their intentions.

"Hi there friend," the lead rider gestured.

Vince gave a quick glance observing as much as he could in the few seconds before answering. All three wore their guns low and the hammer strap had been removed. This set off an alarm and Vince turned sideways and pulling the strap from his hammer in a way they couldn't notice.

"Pushing those horses pretty hard in this heat," Vince remarked.

"In a hurry to meet someone, not that that's any of you're business," the lead rider stated.

Vince noticed the others eyeing him and Colt.

"Nice outfit that horse of yours is courting," the lead rider continued. "All that must have cost a pretty penny."

"Might have, not that it's any of you're business." Vince sarcastically returned.

"You got a pretty smart mouth mister," the rider to the left answered.

Vince knew there was going to be trouble, whether he wanted it or not. They were all in a close bunch and Vince knew this was to his advantage if shooting started. He was standing on the ground which would give him the edge of clearing leather and having steady aim. If shooting started their horses would be darting about, hindering their accuracy. Vince was ready and in no mood for much more or this.

"I think you three are running from something. If that's so you best get while the gettin's good," Vince warned.

But the warning did no good.

"I like your horse. Mine here is tired, I think we'll trade," the lead man stated.

"I think not, now get or whatever is after you will be picking you out of the dirt," was Vince's final warning.

They went for their guns. On a one on one, Vince may have pulled his and showed a man he had no chance, but these were three and his life was threatened.

He pulled his pistol and fanned off three shots.

One of the men was able to get a shot off but a bullet from Vince's gun ripped through the man's shoulder and the man's shot went astray. The other two Vince got off hitting their mark with enough force to send the two off their horses head first into the dirt.

"I give!" yelled the survivor, don't shoot.

While still sitting on his horse, bleeding from the shoulder, Vince walked over and removed the bridle from the man's horse.

"Get or I will," Vince retorted.

Knowing he wouldn't get far before bleeding to death and not being able to make any time without a bridle, the law would be on him in no time. Dead or alive.

He walked around and lifted the bodies of the other two back on their horses tying them to secure the bodies across their saddles. He double checked his ties, not wanting to do it a second time.

Figuring there must be a town near-by from which these three had been running from, he would turn these two over to the authorities.

Reloading his pistol and securing it back in his holster he mounted Colt and hit the trail.

Riding along, thoughts were going through his head wondering what these three might be wanted for. How rough was the country ahead? Would he run into some friends of these three before finding the law?

Colt didn't seem to care. He was content strutting along at his own pace leading two horses carrying two bodies.

Vince was hoping on coming upon a town or meeting-up with a posse before night closed in. He didn't favor entertaining two dead bodies any longer than he had to and surely not over-night at some camp site.

Three hours later again hearing the thunder of horses heading his way, he knew his curiosity was about to be satisfied.

Knowing he was going to have to disclose his name, he thought of letting the two horses go and make a run for the forest off to the right. He knew that would be wrong so he walked the horses along until the pose came into view. The leader was a Deputy Marshal and the rest must have been sworn-in volunteers.

They rode up to him, quickly looking over the cargo he was leading. The Marshal got down off his horse and lifted the dead men's heads by their hair and named each as he did.

"Well I see you saved us a lot of time and trouble," the Marshal said to Vince.

"They tried to rob me of my horse," Vince responded. "No ones gonna take my horse, as they found out."

"Ones missing," the Marshal mentioned.

"You'll find him north about a half days ride. Doubt if he'll be alive. He was bleeding quite heavily and had no reins so I doubt if he'll be too hard to find," Vince confessed.

"What these men do, Marshal, if I may ask?" Vince asked.

"Shot two men and my deputy while he was trying to break up a card game gone wrong," he responded. "Seems these fellas knew how to cheat, but not very well. Where you heading, may I ask?"

"You may. I'm heading to Albuquerque," Vince offered. "I hope I can leave these two with you and carry on."

"There's a reward for these men," the Marshal offered. "If you meet us back in town I'll be sure you get it."

"Thanks, but no thanks," I'd just as soon get on my way. "I am glad you came along when you did so I had the chance to tell my side of the story."

"Very well," he answered hesitantly. "Your name would be?"

Vince remembered the name Jeb used to introduce him.

"Vince, Vince Rodgers," Vince surrendered.

"Where you coming from? Mind If I check up on you?" The Marshal asked.

"Not at all," Alamosa and Sheriff Parker is the name to ask for if you need," Vince responded. "I have nothing to hide."

"I'm sure, but I still have a job to do Mr. Rodgers," answered the Marshal.

Hoping the Sheriff never got around to checking on him back in Colorado, he doubted this one would either. He'd be lucky if he remembered the name he gave as it was. He saw he wasn't writing anything down.

"Albuquerque, huh?" he Marshal repeated. "If I need anything more I wire you."

"Great, nice meeting you all and glad I could help the law," Vince answered honestly.

"You saved us quite a bit of time and trouble. Be on your way and thanks," the Marshal stated.

Turning his horse south he gave a light spur to Colt. The men fell out of sight in minutes.

"That went well," Vince thought to himself.

Thinking it was time to get to Albuquerque without hanging around small towns which had little to offer him except big trouble.

When he got to the next town he planned to find a wagon in good shape to haul supplies and he would head for his destination without any more distractions.

The next afternoon he reached the small town of Espanola. He purchased a wagon with a great work horse that looked strong and lean, just what Vince needed to make good time. From there he headed out with a list of supplies he made ahead of time. Adding to it as he thought of things he may well over looked if he shopped blind.

Deciding to spend the night to get some rest, he'd head-out at the first sign of light. For a few extra dollars he convinced the store keeper to meet him early to help him load and cover the wagon with a new tarp to protect his load from any bad weather he may encounter on his trip.

After an early dinner he sat-in on a few hands of cards. He saw quickly that staying in this town too long was sure to be trouble. The crowd looked rough and ready. Glancing at other tables he noticed every sort of cheating at cards known to man. This was of no concern to him and a while later he grabbed-up his winnings and headed for the hotel early to get some much needed rest.

Washing up he was ready to turn in when there was a slight knock on the door. Cautiously he opened the door with his gun in-hand. Peering out through the gap in the door he saw part of a very pretty red head.

"I noticed you as you were playing cards earlier. When I got time to come over I saw you were gone. My friend told me what room you were in. I thought you might like some company," she explained hopefully.

"I'm sorry Miss but I have to be up early to leave town," he surrendered.

"Let me come in. I won't stay long. I'm sure you could use some serious attention," she begged.

Not having any loving for a long time he opened the door and let her in.

The next morning came fast as usual. He opened his eyes feeling refreshed and ready to go. He looked over to see he was by himself. It wasn't a dream he realized and yourned for more. Darn honest of her to keep her word. Within minutes he was dressed and heading out the door for the stable.

The wagon was there waiting and Colt was bridled and tied to the back. Pulling to the front of the General Store he found the owner waiting as promised. In less than a half hour Vince was slapping the reins and his wagon was heading south to Albuquerque.

He felt good and knew he would find the trail comfortable, for a while. The weather looked good and there was quite a breeze. He wasn't favorable to driving a wagon but he knew he could change back as the load got lighter. Pulling a pack horse with Colt following always seemed to make the trip longer.

Mentally going over his inventory of supplies, he kept a steady pace down the long dusty trail. If there was anything missing now he would just have to do without. What was he going to discover on this trip should keep his mind razor sharp. Not expecting the things he experienced since he left Alamosa, he knew they should act as a lesson to him to stay alert.

Days went by without a hitch. Things were going so well he untied Colt and let him run along on his own, keeping an eye on him not letting him, stray too far from the wagon. Colt began making a game to see just how far he could get before hearing Vince's whistle calling him back. Vince got a kick out of it too. It kept the monotony from getting to him. He knew they still had miles to go, so doing anything out of the ordinary helped. Practicing with his gun was one thing he enjoyed, knowing he wasn't getting any younger he swore to get faster and more accurate. Remembering the day he saw Tillman and Jeb missing each other never strayed from his mind.

He promised that any future gunfight he was involved in he would shoot twice avoiding any chance of the same predicament his best friend experienced. His other thoughts were on the lady who graced him with her company the night before leaving town. Not ever thinking he would be able to let something like that happen, he was glad he did. It was quite a pleasant thought when he started getting stressed and over-tired.

Deer were plenty as they crossed his path many times. Rabbits sat at the edge of greenery picking what they wanted. They would eat until they could eat no more or run to deeper grass when threatened. Vince watched and was amused how nature produced food for its creatures to survive.

Watching a flock of buzzards up ahead, he thought the worst but as he rode closer he could see again nature at work. It was the buzzards that cleaned up and disposed of dead animals, even men on occasion. It was sometimes gruesome but necessary for the balance of nature.

Listening to the horses stepping along the trail, he found himself counting the steps. He would start to sing a song from time to time but didn't know all the words, so never finished any unless finished by his whistling. Colt didn't mind because he knew danger was nowhere when his master was enjoying this meaningless entertainment.

Today they passed no one and no one passed them, just another lonely boring day.

There was no good place to set camp as they became tired so they carried on. Vince didn't really care as long as he wasn't falling over with sleep. It only meant they were cutting miles off their trip.

Everybody needed sleep eventually and after trimming off a few more miles it was time to find a place, even though not secluded, to stop and get some sleep. Steering the wagon closer to the mountain side Vince was lucky enough to find a grassy bushy area to set up camp for the night.

Learning his lesson, he made sure he would have a fire that would last through the night, and keep a glow to keep varmints away. Vince placed the fire close to the wagon as he would be sleeping under it. He sure didn't need to have a rattle snake snug up to him while he slept. He tied the horses close-by, giving them plenty of rein to reach clean green grass, yet close enough to give warning if necessary.

Vince dug out a few biscuits and beef jerky watching the moon and silhouettes of birds and bats while he ate. Tonight he would drink fresh water from a small stream he found near buy.

Soon he was asleep and having his usual dreams of Jane and Richard. He knew in time dreams of this nature would end, but they were pleasant now that he was alone on the trail.

Drinking a hot cup of coffee and cooking bacon the next morning, he figured this would be the day or evening they should be near Albuquerque.

Chapter 21

Johnny West was nearly fifty miles away from Albuquerque. He was thinking now how safe he was far away from Mike Ballard and his ornery jackasses. He was ready for a long drinking binge then having his way with some wild women when he got to town. The thought of steak and potatoes for dinner made his mouth water. Having money, he looked forward to the best room offered at the hotel and clean or new clothes.

He knew he could make enough money playing poker or signing-on as a hired gun which he was also used to. He knew men who lived in Albuquerque but doubted they would still be around. They would probably have been hung by now or running from the law. In Johnnie's line of work it was hard to meet and make friends with respectable men, and when he did it was for the reason to separate them from their money.

Johnny shot his first man when he was fourteen over a sandwich a boy took from him. Since then he was on the wild path and one of the gunfighters lucky to still be alive.

One of the more logical reasons Johnny lived so long was that he played poker more than he hired out as a gun, and he was a good poker player without having to cheat. He was so good he could catch a man cheating triggered by a natural instinct. No one knew his method but he was never wrong once he locked on to a cheater. He was also smart enough to let one of the other players take care of a cheater to keep himself out of trouble unless it was impossible. Then he would step in because of his sureness and poise. With his distinct ways he could make a man freeze. Later getting a reputation with his gun, it was time for him to move around the country, even though never being convicted of a killing.

Johnny wasn't a man without some good qualities. He once found a dead mother wolf with one surviving pup. He raised that pup making quite a pet for himself. He had that wolf for years, staying loyal to the man who saved him. Johnny took him everywhere. He would bring him into saloons while he drank or sit-in for some poker. The wolf would always lay at his feet and be his security. If asked to remove the wolf he would always give the same response, "ask me again and you'll be drinking from a dog bowl," that would usually be the end of it. Only once did a man who didn't take the hint, found himself looking down Johnny's gun barrel.

Johnny had that wolf for three years. Then one evening he got into a scuffle with a man and the wolf attacked the aggressor. The man pulled his gun. Johnny grasped the man's gun but it was too late, it went off, killing the wolf. Johnny pulled the gun away smashing it to the side of the man's face, killing him just as if he had just shot him. The Sheriff came and not knowing the whole story tried to arrest him so Johnny shot him, picked up his wolf and left town to bury it. Forced to keep going since he was now a wanted man.

Ironically Johnny had a brother who was the Sheriff in Baker City, Oregon. He had told Johnny that if they ever met-up he would have no choice but to arrest and hang him. Johnny knew if the day came he would have to shoot his brother, so he made a point to stay out of Oregon.

Sheriff Charlie West was no slouch with a gun, and it was a fact he was the one who taught Johnny how to shoot. They were brought up by their mother, not ever knowing their father. Word had it he was caught and tortured by Indians when the boys were very small. Their mother refused to talk much about it. They had a younger sister also but never kept in touch after their mother died.

Johnny became a loner with very few friends. The ones he did have would betray him more than not, so he continued life with no room for trust for any man. He always had money and if he didn't he knew how to get it. If he was in a town where he didn't care to take chances he would get it at poker tables. If not he would hire out as a gunman or rob a bank, train or gold exchange office, rarely leaving witnesses.

Chapter 22

Riding into Albuquerque Vince found it to be a pretty big town. Not knowing how long he would be staying he took a room at the Atlantis Hotel paying for it by the night. If he could get comfortable and do well at the poker tables he figured he may stay a while. He wanted to wire Jeb and see if there was any news that would have importance to him. Everything depended on something now in Vince's life.

The town may have been bigger than most but the familiar piano was the same as any other town. He drove the wagon over to the livery and paid generously to have the horses taken care of. He offered to share the profits from the wagon and supplies still left. The keeper was used to this and always looked for a way for a few extra bucks. Vince offered a couple more coins to oil his saddle and bridal. This was a man Vince knew he could trust watching him approach and handle Colt. He gave no resistance to the mans moves which surprised Vince knowing Colt didn't take well to strangers.

It seemed no time at all before he was washed with a belly full and on his way to play some poker. Walking into the salon he could see there were more than enough tables and figured within hours they would all be occupied. He found a table of his liking to the back of the room with a vacant chair facing the door.

"Mind if I set in boys?" he asked politely.

"Not at all mister, sit," one well dressed man answered.

"My name is Vince," he offered.

"What's your business?" another of the men asked immediately.

"Just drifting," Vince responded.

The others went around the table introducing themselves, but the one Vince was interested in was the man named Colin. He seemed to jump right in and ask his business in town.

He had a look about him, young, wealthy, card player and possibly a shootist. He would pay special attention to this gentleman on this evening.

He found the other men knew and liked this fellow playing cards often with them. This put Vince a little more at ease but he would still stay cautious until he knew everything he could about him.

The talk was small and the cards were falling his way immediately, at least for the first few hands. This put Vince on guard watching the shuffling and dealing more closely. He saw nothing and took it this was not going to be one of his better nights. He lost the suspicion any sat back and enjoyed the company not caring if it meant losing a few hands. These men were good and he welcomed the challenge. A few more hands and the cards began falling his way again. Then as fast as it changed, it changed back. He had a great time playing and visiting with these men knowing that they were honest. At the end of the night he excused himself and found himself invited to join them the next evening. He graciously accepted and actually was looking forward to it.

This was a town he knew he could like. Looking around the room he saw many attractive women. Men acting like gentlemen, laughing, talking, and taking a break from what ever they do during the day. All in all, the atmosphere was quite nice. He was looking forward to a good nights sleep in a nice comfortable bed.

Morning would come fast and he would be checking out the quality of breakfast. Wanting to get a telegram off to Jeb he would hope to hear back in a couple of days.

Walking to leave he was almost run into a Deputy Marshal.

"Good evening, Marshal," Vince gestured.

Seeing a Deputy Marshal he figured there would be at least two deputies also, making this a fairly safe town.

Just as he got to the batwings a pretty young girl walk up and invited her self to have breakfast with him in the morning.

"Would be honored," Vince replied. "But only if you keep me warm tonight.

The woman intertwined her arm with Vince and let him lead her away.

The rooms were quite large, Vince always got a room facing the street to know what was going on at all times. He could always check out how busy the streets were by just looking out a window. Street windows always proved safer as any smart intruder would know trying to come in through a street side window put him in total visibility of people on the street.

The next morning Vince kept his promise and escorted his newly found friend to a nice breakfast. The coffee was very good and very hot. He enjoyed the company as he listened and got to know his new friend Sally. She would be his new contact for information as well as companionship but promised himself that's all it would be. He excused himself and headed for the telegraph office. The sooner he got a note off to Jeb, the sooner he'd get a response.

Chapter 23

Letting his horse walk at his own speed gave Johnny a chance to gaze around as he rode down Main Street. He was hungry so he pulled up and tied his horse off in front of the saloon.

The room was not too crowded and he found a hot cup of coffee waiting for him as he sat. The aroma from the room was great and he couldn't wait to shovel a pile of hot cakes into his empty stomach. Hot cakes came almost as fast as his coffee. He really didn't care as he was enjoying his coffee and a cigarette watching around the room noticing what everyone else was eating. After devouring the hot cakes he sat back to another enjoyable coffee and rolled another cigarette. He was in no hurry so savored the comfort and people chatting from some of the occupied tables, trying to pick up on any news that might be of any interest to him. A while later it was time for him to bring his horse to the livery and get a room for the next few days. He hoped he would find an acquaintance or two from when he stayed here before.

Leaving his horse off he gave instructions to the stableman of how he wanted his horse taken care of, paying him in advance with quite a tip to know he would do him well.

When all of a sudden out of the corner of his eyes he noticed a real fancy oiled down saddle and bridle slung over a saddle bench. He couldn't believe what he was seeing.

"Hey mister," he yelled. "Who belongs to the fancy saddle?"

"Don't know his name, he got in late yesterday afternoon," the tender answered as he was getting ready to shoe a horse.

"Can you describe him?" Johnny asked.

"Can't say I can, but his holster matched the saddle," he offered.

"That should make it easier," Johnny thought to himself.

This was bad for Vince for he had no idea someone came into town and stumbled on the where about of Vince Masters, and wouldn't know the person if he walked right into him on the boardwalk.

Johnny was already figuring how well he'd be awarded by Mike if he was able to wire him and tell him he killed the man who killed his brother. He knew that until that task was done he had to keep everything to himself. He would look around tonight at the saloon; see what he was up against, not that it mattered. Johnny was pretty sure of his abilities with a gun to even think there could be a real challenge.

Vince stayed in his room most of the day after breakfast. Taking out his gun cleaning tools, he began to dismantle and give them the hours it took to clean them correctly. He had neglected them long enough. These were his life, cleaning guns on the trail was impossible. There were too many small parts when dismantling a gun and if one fell into the dirt it was over. Doing it on a clean uncluttered table was the safe and smart way to clean them. When he was done with the pistols he grabbed his rifle and went on to clean it also. When done he inserted cartridges in all the guns and refilled the holster.

With nothing else planned he walked over to the livery to see if his saddle and bridle were done. The workmanship on that saddle superceded itself when it was oiled and polished out. Not wanting to leave such a fine saddle to temp thieves he decided to bring it and the bridle back to his room.

He skipped lunch so figured he'd rest up til dinner then head to the saloon and hoped to meet up with the same men he met the night before. He laid his head back on the pillow and was out like a light. He woke like and alarm clock. It was six o'clock. He swung his legs out and stood up in one swift movement. A quick wash and off he went, hungry as all get out. He couldn't imagine why he would miss lunch and swore he'd not do that again. Adjusting his eyes to the brightness he swung his gun belt around his waist, buckled it and headed down stairs.

The dining room was filling up, but he found his usual table to be vacant and waiting for him. A cute little brunette came to the table with a cup of coffee and silverware.

"Good evening sir," she said in a soft voice.

"To you too mam, call me Vince, please," Vince responded.

"Ok Vince, you can call me Carol," she answered back. "It's really Carolyn but I like Carol."

"Fine then Carol, how about a nice rare steak with the fixings," Vince ordered.

"Great, hope you can eat it all," she teased.

"I missed lunch, so I'm sure I will," he assured her.

It wasn't long before she was back at his table with a plate full, along with a pot of coffee.

"Leave it," Vince asked nodding to the pot of coffee.

"Great, enjoy," Carol invited.

When Vince pushed the plate way it was polished clean as he wiped the remains with his last piece of bread. He then leaned back in his chair and rolled a cigarette, lit it and let all that devoured food begin digesting.

Carol came by to see if he needed anything but he kindly declined, and went about watching the people around him. It wasn't that busy he needed to give up his table so he just sat and savored the moment.

When people started to clear out he knew it was time to start to think of moving to the saloon for some card playing, but he amused himself with the thought the room wasn't that cleared out. So he continued to sit. He watched Carol clear tables and bring coffee to patrons and thought how attractive she was, but caught him self before thinking of trying anything. He knew she was a good women and not in the saloon business to sell her services. Yet she would give him a sweet sexy smile and wink when she caught him looking at her. Vince felt a warm feeling and let himself accept all the friendliness she would offer.

Finally he knew it was time leave with hope of finding his same chair vacant and waiting in the salon.

Walking in he looked straight for the table he played at the night before and sure enough it was vacant with the same men already throwing cards down. He gave a Panasonic look around the room and then preceded to joins his acquaintances.

What he didn't know was there was someone else watching men coming though the bat doors. Someone who was looking more at gun belts than faces.

"Good evening gentlemen," Vince announced.

"Good evening, Vince," one man answered, remembering his name.

"Back to donate some of that big money you took from us," Colin teased.

"Yeah, sure," Vince responded. "If you call that big money you have no business gambling. You should stay home with your wife and kids."

Just then Sally showed up with beer for everyone.

"Good evening Vince," she greeted in the same sexy voice as the night before.

All the men kind of looked at Sally then to Vince with a puzzled look.

"You got something going with Sally no one knows about?" one of the men, Ben asked after Sally walked out of hearing range.

"Now wouldn't that be between me and the lady?" Vince responded.

"You just gave us your answer," Ben retorted while shuffling the cards. "Five card?"

"Fine with us, deal," Colin ordered.

The evening of card playing, talking, joking and winning or losing had begun.

Two hands in Vince commenced to roll a cigarette. This town and the people in it seemed all right. He may have to stick around a while, he felt very comfortable and at peace here.

From time to time he would let his eyes cover as much of the saloon they would allow. He looked over the men at the bar but saw nothing that should alarm him or grab his curiosity.

The piano player stopped only to gulp done some beer or listen to some one ask him to play a certain song. He was good and seemed tireless. Vince thought how great it was for someone to enjoy his job so much.

As the night before no one was raking in large sums of winnings which would make for a long enjoyable evening.

Glancing up toward the bar to see if he could catch a glimpse of Sally he noticed a man looking over his way. Not just looking but staring for seconds. This got Vince's attention and he immediately brought his guard up. Maybe he was taking this a bit too seriously, but this was how a man survived to live a long life and he had no plans of seeing it shortened by not being cautious. This was one thing Jeb taught him when they first started traveling together and he wouldn't forget it.

He started watching out of the corner of his eye and begin thinking he was being silly. No one knew him here and he hadn't caught the man looking since. It was his deal and as he shuffled the cards he forgot the man at the bar.

Sally came over from time to time serving each man his choice of beer or whiskey, and each time Vince would get a nudge or a wink. This embarrassed him in front of the guys, not that they were paying any attention.

Not having any concept of time Vince finally noticed the saloon was thinning out. The piano player was finished for the night closing the key cover and finishing his last beer. Even the man that aroused Vince was gone.

"Well, I guess I'm gonna call it a night," Ben announced

"Me too," Colin followed, scraping up all the bills in front of him and making a neat pile before folding them to fit his coat pocket.

Well the night was over. Vince had another great evening, so great he didn't notice whether he won or lost. But as Sally was waiting for him when he went to leave he knew he had won. Money wasn't every thing. A nice warm body next to him for the night was. Not knowing or caring he was up almost two hundred dollars, also. Walking up the street neither could expel the romantic light the moon was laying over the area. The hotel was deserted as they walked in and headed for the stairs, so deserted Vince took to defense mode right away, but soon found out there was no reason for alarm. It was just a coincidence that everyone had turned in earlier. Minutes after they had entered and closed them selves in others were heard walking the halls. Vince relaxed looking forward to enjoy his company.

CHAPTER 24

Down at the end of the hall Johnny West was relaxing in his room being entertained by his own visitor of the evening.

Seeing the wanted posters he was sketched with a full beard and mustache, seeing this he had gone to his room and shaved as clean as he could. By wearing his hat lower than usual he was faintly recognizable.

Though his mind was on his newly found friend for the night, he was also thinking with his devious mind of how he would eliminate the man with the fancy saddle. He knew who his adversary was, now he had to find a way to get him to face him man to man, gun to gun. He was a wanted man and knew if he attracted any attention or stayed too exposed someone could recognize him and he would be in for the fight of his life.

He decided that he would lay low for the next couple of days and see if he could find a pattern in Vince's routine.

Johnny wasn't a back shooter, this whole thing was a coincidence coming to the same town Vince decided to come to. Neither man had a real reason to come here but it happened. Now there would be a gun fight and one of them would be eliminated. Johnny decided to take Vince's saddle bridle gun belt and guns for his trophy. It would also be proof to Mike Ballard he shot the man who killed his brother, even though he wasn't sure he wanted anything to do with Mike or his fellow gun fighters again.

Trying real hard to get all this out of his mind, he turned to his evening companion and enjoyed himself as well as giving her the attention she craved for.

Later that night laying there sleepless he also thought this was a pretty nice town.

Tomorrow he hoped to get to play some poker and give his other interest a rest for a few days. Thinking of the ways he would like this all to go down he found him self having a body snuggle up to him enticing himself to fall into a dead sleep.

The morning woke everyone with a heavy rain beating on the roof. Johnny got up and looked out the window to find the streets already muddying up with puddles and the sky showing no end of rain in sight. This enticed him to crawl back into bed with his honey and get a few more hours sleep. Breakfast was never important to Johnny which showed by his tall lanky body. Come lunch time he would make up for it.

Vince got up and got dressed letting Sally sleep. He wanted to go down to the livery and check on Colt. When he returned he would wake Sally and they would go down to eat.

Walking into the stable he found the blacksmith nailing on a set of shoes on the largest horse he had seen in this town. Seeing Vince walk in he stopped and greeted him.

"Well, it looks like a good day to stay dry and get caught up on chores," Vince kidded.

"Yeah, nobody will be going out in this weather, so I spect they'll be comin in asking for all kinds of favors," he responded.

"I thought I'd let you know I came back the other day and picked up my bridle and saddle, you made it look real nice," Vince commended flipping him a silver dollar.

"Not that it's any of my business mister but a man came in here the other day and asked what I knew about the owner of that saddle," the blacksmith offered.

"What you tell him?" Vince asked.

"By the time I caught myself I told him if he found the gun belt that matched the saddle he found the man he was looking for," he answered embarrassing. "Later I saw the saddle gone but the horse was still here, so I figured you came and got it."

Vince looked around then walked over to Colt. As usual Colt's ears picked up when he saw Vince. After treating him to a few handful of oats and clean water Vince proceeded to leave.

"You ain't mad at me mister are ya?" the smith asked.

"No, don't worry about it, if he didn't find out from you he would have found out by someone else," he responded. "I'm just wondering who and why some ones asking about me. I guess time will tell. What did this fella look like?"

"Young, good lookin fella, blond hair and a beard," he reported.

The one thing he didn't know was that Johnny had shaved since he saw him last.

Vince started back getting drenched doing so. He was thinking with every step of who he may have seen that would have stayed in his mind. The only man he thought of was the man he caught staring at him from the bar the other night. But he didn't think he could remember him again if he saw him. He didn't even remember if he had a beard or not. From now on he will remember any face that strikes him suspicious. Now it could mean life or death.

When he walked to the door Sally opened it simultaneously.

"Heard you coming down the hall," she confessed. "I'd know that walk any where. Come on, I'm hungry."

Not having to go out side it was appreciated by both. Finding a table that gave a full view to the room Vince and Sally took a seat.

Carol walked over and Vince saw a different attitude immediately. He felt bad and knew why she was acting the way she was. He would stop by later and explain his actions but for right now he was in a embarrassing spot and would have to live with it.

Carol service was still punctual and professional but she couldn't have been colder to Vince. There was no small talk, no winks and sexy smiles.

Vince looked up to see another couple walk in the opposite side of the room. They were a handsome couple and Vince lost interest in them quickly and went back to give his attention to Sally. Feeling uncomfortable over the situation with Carol, he didn't sit around much longer after finishing breakfast. Normally he would have enjoyed two more cups of coffee, but not this morning. When Carol left to go fetch an order for another customer, Vince and Sally left.

Walking from the room Vince gave a quick glance over to the couple on the other side of the room, but found neither paying any attention him.

Not knowing Johnny was paying mind to Vince but only because most of Johnny's glances were quick and out from the corner of his eyes.

Later Vince walked back to see Carol and see what was on her mind. After some fast talking and finding some convincing compliments, Vince had talked Carol to take a ride with him out to the country and get to know each other better.

Johnny noticed and suspected Vince was on to him. Why he didn't show more clues confused Johnny but he would keep his guard up like he knew Vince would be doing. He may make his move now sooner than he wanted. He was figuring on challenging Vince to a gunfight, kill him and high tail it out of town. The one thing he wanted though was Vince's horse saddle and gear. With luck Vince would take a ride outside of town and he would be ready. Not knowing but Vince had promised Carol a ride this day but the rain foiled it. If Johnny was on the ball he would find that the ride was planned for the next day.

The next day came soon and Johnny was alert enough to see Vince and Carol heading to the stables. Packing up his gear as fast as he could without missing the direction Vince and Sally rode out. He had no intentions of returning to town after challenging Vince. He had no intentions of killing a woman, so he would have to think of what he would do with her after killing Vince. It would be dangerous to leave her alive knowing she could recognize him but he also knew he was no women killer.

Chapter 25

Vince and Carol rode out about three miles when they found the perfect spot to stop and spend some private time together. Today the sun was full and bright with a small breeze to keep it comfortable.

"Oh Vince, this is such beautiful country, you're the first man to bring me out here."

"I feel honored, mam," Vince answered. "I glad you found it in yourself to let me bring you out here. I know you don't like Sally, but your way too much of a lady, and I know that. Sally does what she does and it isn't the same life you've chosen for yourself. What I don't understand why a beautiful woman like your self isn't spoken for."

"That's real nice to hear Vince, but I was married before. My husband was shot down in cold blood in an attempted bank robbery right here in this town. I just haven't been able to bring myself to betray what we had by marrying another." She conceded.

"He was a real good man Vince. I knew I'd never find anyone as good as he was. Not until I met you, you're a kind man, I knew that the day I met you. I watched your actions and manners. You were brought up different than most. You're a hard man Vince, but you have a soft side you can't hide."

"That may be so Carol, but when I get close to someone I love things happen. I won't let myself get close to anyone again. I have undesirable men to find, and when I do I will kill them. You might think bad of me to say such a thing but it will be kill or be killed, and I think even you understand what I'm saying."

"I understand Vince, so I'll not push myself on you," she promised. "I'm not that kind."

"Well if I do look for a wife you better look out," Vince teased. "You'd be my choice."

Carol liked to hear that, it made her all tingly inside, and knew he said that to do so.

The sun that had been bathing them for hours disappeared and in seconds reappeared. Looking up the two could see that clouds were building.

"We better get back, honey," Carol said. "If we leave now we may get back without getting wet."

Vince grabbed Carol, giving her a big kiss and hard hug.

"You're right as usual, let's get," Vince agreed.

Vince when over and grabbed the reins of the two horses and led them over to where Carol was standing.

There behind him was the familiar sound of a hammer being pulled back.

That sound immediately gave a bad feeling to Vince's stomach. He could see in the eyes of Carol he didn't have to turn to see that they were in trouble.

Slowly turning around he found him self facing a young man with a .45 pointing at him from the man's hip.

"Fancy horse you have there mister," Johnny said.

"You have a name?" Vince asked. "I should a least be introduced to the man who wants my horse."

"My name is Johnny West and it's not you horse I want. I'm here to kill you and after you're dead you won't have any use for him, so I may as well have him." Johnny confessed. "What's your name since we're introducing ourselves?"

"You don't know my name and you say you're here to kill me?" Vince questioned.

"I've been hired by Mike Ballard," Johnny responded.

"So that's it, but I didn't kill him, he was only wounded," Vince retorted. "He was murdered in jail so he wouldn't talk."

"I'm not the judge, just the executioner," Johnny exclaimed.

"Mike Ballard huh?" Vince asked. "So his brother hired you. He's not man enough so he hired a gunman to do his dirty work?"

"What's it to you? Johnny answered. "He paid me, now I have a job to do."

"Do I get a chance or are you gonna shot me in cold blood?" Vince asked.

Johnny slowly placed his gun back into his holster.

"There that better?" Johnny challenged.

"Yeah, one more thing though," Vince asked. "Was it Jake Ballard who hired you to kill me?"

"You may as well know it was," Johnny asked.

Carol was standing froze watching all this in horror.

The two men were facing each other in a fair gunfight. Vince felt a lot better knowing that a least he wasn't going to get shot without a fair chance.

"Can I ask you one more thing?" Vince asked. "Where's this Jake Ballard now, does he know who I am?"

"East, he thought that was the way you went, and no, he only knows your horse and saddle." Johnny answered.

"Enough talk," Johnny retorted.

Vince knew this was it. He was watching his eyes and upper body looking for a flinch.

It came, giving Vince the chance to beat his draw.

The blast from the gun pushed flame from the gun as well as the lead.

Vince stood there realizing he wasn't shot and immediately saw the blood stain finding its way growing through Johnny's shirt.

Falling to his knees, Johnny knew he was way to slow. He cleared leather but never got a shot off. Falling forward on his face he knew he was dying fast.

Carol gave out a short scream, running to Vince where they both watched Johnny expel his last breath.

"I think I'm gonna be sick," she warned, squeezing the breath out of him.

Now it was too late the rain started to come down lightly.

This certainly wasn't the way Vince wanted to end the day with Carol. This wasn't the way he wanted to end any day. He was happy that Carol wasn't hurt in any way and that he was the victor in a gunfight with a person he never met or heard of.

Johnny was as big as Vince so it took some doing get his body up and laid over his saddle. He was glad to be able to get a man of his size on the horse. There was no way he would want to ask Carol to help him lift a dead man onto his horse. He even asked Carol to stand off to the side so she wouldn't have to witness any unpleasantness.

It was still raining lightly as they headed back to town. He gave Carol his coat to stay as dry as possible. He didn't want her to get sick and lose time from her job.

When they rode back to town men circled the horses showing their curiosity to find what had happened. Vince stopped in front of the hotel and escorted Carol to her room so she could change and warm up. Leaving her to do so he went back to head for the sheriff office, only to find the sheriff already standing at the horses.

"I'll need a statement on what happened out there but the man here is Johnny West. He's wanted in four states and has a thousand dollar bounty on him," the sheriff announced.

"Give the reward to Carol, Sheriff," Vince responded. "She just went through quite an ordeal. She can get that house at the end of the street she's been talking about."

"It's your decision, I'll make sure she gets the money," the sheriff promised.

Vince had no idea how she would react when she was given the money, but one thing for sure was he was heading east as fast as he could. He had someone to catch up to. He was to avenge the man who arranged to have his family killed if not involved himself.

He went about his way to get things packed and ready. He would leave without even a good by. He owed no one any explanation. He liked this town and the people he had met, but now he had to leave to take care of business he now found without even looking. Vince wasn't a superstitious man but he always thought if he was to find the killers of his wife and son it would be with the help of his now passed away love.

CHAPTER 26

It was close to midnight when Vince mounted Colt and headed out of town. He rode the back street so he wouldn't have to pass the hotel or saloon. He thought how much he would miss the company of his poker playing friends, the warmth of his friend Sally and the companionship of his friend Carol.

It was all good but two of the three were heading in a direction Vince wasn't ready to take.

The moon wasn't quite over-head, and full enough to give him plenty of riding time. He knew he could finish the night, and then ride all day. A soft breeze was keeping the temperature comfortable for himself and Colt.

He would venture north-east and see where that would lead him. He knew there weren't many towns along the way, so no straight path would be needed.

Santo Domingo would be his next town which was about a two day ride. Remembering what Johnny West said about Jake holding up a while to see if he had gotten ahead of himself. How long ago was that? Figuring he was probably heading back to Arkansas, he would be in no hurry. If that was to be true, he knew they would be meeting up sooner or later anyway. If only Johnny stayed alive long enough to give him some specifics. Then again, he was lucky Johnny spilled any information. That was strictly against outlaw standards.

He tried to shed some of his anger. He was on a mission to rid the world of bad men who fed on weak families. He didn't want to stray from his plan, his obsession. It was only natural he wanted to meet-up with Jake, but not kill Colt in the process of trying to catch up. His adversaries would be around, making trouble, spending money, not worrying of their destiny 'til it was their time, so why should he push it?

Arriving in Santo Domingo, he found it to be somewhat of a dirty town. He found a hotel to clean the trail dust and give Colt a rest. The saloon seemed to be different from most as the bar was off to one side rather straight back from the bat doors. Making himself visible was the only plan he had to see if any one was interested in him. No one was, but a man was interested in his horse and his attire. Unaware that anything was going to happen, Vince ordered a beer, and took a couple of long slugs and enjoyed the feeling as it washed down several days of trail dust.

"Mister, mister," a man anxiously called to Vince. "There's a man outside looking at your horse. I think he's gonna take it from you."

Looking over to see a small Mexican man, he chuckled, swallowed the rest of his beer, threw some coin on the bar, then ordered a beer for his informant.

Vince pushed the doors open to exit onto the walkway. Sure enough there was a man mounting Colt. He already had him untied and pushed back. The man paid Vince no mind as he spurred Colt for his get away. What he got was the ride of his life. Vince nonchalantly pulled a paper, rolled a cigarette, and watched enjoying the whole fiasco. Colt was relatively easy on this fellow in the beginning but the more he felt the spurs in his sides the more determined he was out to throw down the rider. Lighting the Cigarette, he stepped down off the walk way and made his way over to the man who just finished a nose dive into the street.

Knowing this man was in no condition to defend him self, he walked over and pulled him up by his collar. He saw the man was wearing his gun tied low. A gunfighter thinking he was going to walk-up and ride off with a man's horse. Boy! Did he pick the wrong horse.

Someone had alerted the sheriff and he was on his way. Vince only had seconds to get any satisfaction, so he pulled back and smashed the man's face as hard as he dared. Stealing a horse was a hanging offense. Vince wanted his own small part of personal justice before the man was dragged off to jail.

"You just rode in, mister?" the sheriff asked.

"Yes sir, just about a half hour ago," Vince responded.

"Well that's the kind of horse anyone in this town would want. I can see there's gonna be a lot of trouble. It's lucky there wasn't a gunfight. Even though this man is gonna hang for this, gunfire won't be tolerated. I suggest you get what business you have here done and head out," the sheriff warned.

The sheriff was not very friendly and Vince took a disliking to him immediately. He was the victim, being talked to like a criminal because he was fortunate enough to have a fancy horse and gear.

Vince walked back into the saloon to find the man who had warned him at the bar still drinking.

"Thanks mister," Vince praised again.

"You already thanked me," the man returned, "but if you think that guy will spend even an hour in jail, you'd just be kidding yourself. That sheriff is as crooked as the other fellow. It wouldn't surprise me to find out the sheriff paid him to take your horse."

"Is that so," Vince responded in disgust. "Well I'll find out. I'll go back in awhile and see for myself. If it's true, you're gonna see a big change in this town."

"If you did, you'd be doing this town a big favor," the man returned. "He came here about two months ago and we don't know where our sheriff went. He just disappeared. This guy comes into the saloon one Saturday night and announces he was the new sheriff. He had an entourage of four men with him, so he got no objections. The town has had big problems since."

"As I just said we'll see," Vince announced.

He drank a couple more beers with this fellow who called himself Ray. That would be all he needed to stay sharp. Just in case there was any truth to what Ray had just told him he decided to back off on the drinking.

Ray left after a quick good bye. Vince turned to the barkeep to see if there was any truth to what just got said. Having the story confirmed Vince instantly got a negative attitude.

That was good enough for Vince. He finished his beer and turned heel to the bat doors and headed to the sheriff's office.

Walking out to the street, he decided to visit the sheriff's office and see if he could verify that these stories. He didn't have to wait long. As he was fifty feet out, the man who just attempted to steal his horse came out of the sheriff's office. Looking around he caught sight of Vince walking his way. This was his chance to get back at Vince for what he did. Twisting his body so he was face to face with Vince, immediately put Vince into a defense mode. He reached with his thumb and pulled the leather strap from the hammer of his pistol and waited.

The sheriff walked out just as the man went for his gun. Again Vince was faster and as the echo of his gun sounded through the streets the aggressor was already falling to the dirt.

Vince slid his pistol back into his holster and watched the sheriff walk over to the man. He used his foot to roll the body over to confirm his demise.

"I guess you can come with me now mister," the sheriff said.

"I don't think so, sheriff, you saw it was a clear case of self defense," Vince responded.

"That's right," retorted two other men who also witnessed the duel.

"No body asked you," the sheriff yelled to the two men. "Now clear out before I bring you in as accessories," the sheriff warned.

"Stay right there, men," Vince retorted.

"You're resisting arrest?" the sheriff asked Vince.

"There's no reason for an arrest, he drew first and I defended myself," Vince responded. "There's also two witnesses to back me up."

"Have it you're way," the sheriff said as he turned to confront Vince.

"It doesn't have to be this way," Vince warned.

"Maybe not, but you just killed my cousin and what these men say don't count in this town," the sheriff said.

"I say different. So pull the gun or pull that badge and give it to someone who respects the law," Vince warned.

Many people now lined the streets with hopes to see justice served. Here was a man who wasn't as scared as the rest.

"Last chance," the sheriff warned.

"No, it's your last chance. The badge or go for you're gun," Vince retorted, standing his ground.

"Have it you're way," the sheriff said.

His hand was already massaging the grip of his pistol as Vince was well aware.

Vince saw his arm flinch letting him know he was going for his gun.

Vince went for his and in one smooth motion, slid the gun from his holster, cocked it with is thumb, pulled it level and fired. All before the sheriff had begun leveling his gun.

The crowd knew they were now rid of this troublesome sheriff who stood there for seconds before his gun slipped from his hand and fell to the street. He stood a few seconds more starring at Vince in disbelief. Then fell to his knees.

"Sorry sheriff, but the people want a new election for new law in this town," he announced.

He wasn't sure the sheriff heard a thing as he saw his eyes clouding up. The man was already dead. The body didn't know it yet. Finally he fell over onto his face, kicked once, then laid still.

"There's still his other two deputies," a voice in the crowd said.

"Let them come. I can wait," Vince announced.

It wasn't long 'til bullets were flying wildly into the crowd.

This is how the sheriff kept his power. Keep everyone scarred. There wouldn't be any resistance to his rule over the town.

"Everyone take cover," Vince yelled to the crowd.

Taking cover, he gave a quick glance to see if he could see where the shooting was coming from.

"Just step out here," a voice yelled out.

Vince knew it was aimed to him.

"I'm coming out, don't shoot and let's make it fair fight," Vince yelled.

"We're waiting," was the answer.

Walking out, Vince saw the two men standing there. Close together, just as Vince would want them, making the target easier.

Standing twenty feet away Vince kept his hand close and ready. He was hoping some of the crowd would have the grit to come out and stand by him. These two would be arrested and the law would take care of them. No one moved. He knew there was going to be a fight.

"It doesn't have to go down this way," Vince warned. "Unbuckle your gun belts and let them drop.

"Don't think that's gonna happen," the one said.

"This is the man who killed Johnny," a voice came from the side.

Vince glanced over to see a dark well dressed young man wearing a gun, tied low, on his right leg. He was rolling a cigarette nonchalantly leaning against the porch pole.

"He's also the man who killed Kid Stevens some time back in Whitewater," the man stated.

"I don't believe you," one of the deputies responded.

"You see the saddle on this man's horse? There's only one like it in the country that nice," the man stated further. "It used to belong to Stevens."

The two deputies looked at each other and then back at Vince. His eye's squinting directly at them, waiting for their next move.

"Ok. We'll drop our belts," one said already unbuckling.

"You!" Vince addressed the man standing on the walk, "Take these two and lock them up. Send a wire to the next town and have them send a Deputy Marshall. Let him figure all this out."

"What are we supposed to do without a sheriff in town?" another man asked.

"Looks like you've been without one for some time," Vince retorted. "Maybe you can ask this young man to step-in until help arrives."

The kid looked at him showing disapproval as he pushed one of the two deputies toward the jail. Vince followed, seeing he was going to have to convince this fella to do the town's justice.

Once in the office with the two locked-up Vince thanked him and said he would be the only one who could do the job of law man. Tom Jamison was his name. He agreed to do it for a short time since he grew up in town and knew what the citizens had been going through. Tom was just visiting his mother for a short spell and planned of going back north where he was homesteading. Vince gave his first name only, and wasn't asked for his last. They shook hands, and left it at that to prevent another lie. He was getting used to the last name of Rodgers.

"You know, if you grew up here and obviously everyone knows you, being sheriff wouldn't be such a bad job. Why not consider it?" Vince inquired.

"You don't know anything about me," Tom explained. "I killed a man here a few years back. A card cheater, and even though I was cleared, he was liked in this town. More than I, so I was the one to leave and never come back. I only come back to see my Mom and so far no ones bothered me. I'd just assume keep it that way. I have no idea how they'll accept me for deputy. Even if it should be for a short time. So if they have someone they'd rather have, there won't be any argument with me."

"Well one thing's for sure, the people of this town saw you prevent more blood shed here today. That should count for something." Vince conceded. "It was nice to make you're acquaintance Tom. I noticed you wear your gun pretty low. Don't you think that sends a wrong message to the people around here?"

"I hope it does. It keeps them thinking. I'd just a soon keep it that way," Tom answered. "And I can use if I need to. I just hope I never do."

"You sound like an honest man Tom. Good luck," Vince said and he reached out to shake his hand.

CHAPTER 27

Vince was glad to get back on the trail again. Not looking forward to sleeping under the stars after relaxing in a warm comfortable bed, he had time to make up and he wasn't going to get where he needed by contemplating.

Colt on the other hand was ready. There was no wagon packed with supplies. There wasn't even a pack horse. There would be towns scattered on his way where he could get necessary supplies or spend a night in a fairly comfortable bed should the weather change for the worse. Colt would have free rein whenever he wanted and could travel at his own pace. That is unless Vince needed him for something other than what was on Colt's mind.

Vince never did receive a reply from Jeb. Which meant he must not have been in town while Vince was there waiting. He would try again in the next town if he decided to lay up for a few days.

Vince thought back to when he first met Jeb. He had traveled so long, so far, remembering the adventures they experienced. He started wondering if Tom would have been the same kind of traveling companion. Vince remembered Tom saying he wore his gun low for a reason and that he could use it too. Those were the same words Jeb told Vince when they met.

Vince had met friends under disastrous circumstances who would stay with him for the rest of his life even if they weren't with him anymore.

Three days on the trail, Vince noticed the weather beginning to cool. Fall was coming and the biggest clue was in the evenings. He was hoping he could reach some smaller towns early. He knew he would be back to his dad's ranch before winter and wondered what he was going to find when he got there.

He snapped out of his day dreaming when he heard something or someone up ahead. Colts ears perked-up, alerting Vince he indeed did hear something.

The first thing that came to Vince's mind was Jake Ballard. Stopping Colt, he slowly dismounted and ran his hand down Colt's nose to let him know he did a good job. Looking for the closest cover should he need it, he made sure he was ready for anything. Leading Colt over to some nearby tree cover, he stood completely still and listened. He pulled his rifle from its sheath but didn't dare lever a shell into the camber thinking it would alert anyone who might be too close and sneaking up on him.

Then he heard it again. It was definitely someone coming up from behind. Vince stood his ground and watched with intensity. Soon, he saw a silhouette of a horse and rider. The rider was being very cautious. Vince could see his horse had alerted him as Colt did by raising his ears. Raising his rifle he drew a bead on the rider and tried faking him out.

"Hold it right there. I have you covered. Identify yourself. Do it now," Vince warned.

He quickly levered the rifle to let the rider know he meant business.

"I'm the Territorial Deputy Marshall," the man exclaimed.

"Ok. Come out in the open. I'm just passing through and being very cautious." Vince responded.

"Excuse me if I don't show myself just yet. I wasn't born yesterday and sure don't need to take lead by being stupid," was the answer.

"I'm coming out, but I hope to trust you'll have a badge to show me," Vince responded.

"I can do that but all I have is your word," the Marshall said.

Vince figured he was dealing with the real thing so he slid his rifle back into the sheath but kept his hand close to his pistol.

The Marshall was a big man who looked like he could handle himself in a fight. He looked to be in his thirties and wore his gun higher than usual. The badge was visible enough. It did a lot of talking when keeping the peace was required.

He had a pleasant voice and Vince relaxed some as he approached.

"Where you heading?" Vince asked.

"Santa Domingo got a telegraph a few days ago there was an ongoing problem with the law. It all came to an end with the Sheriff and his deputies either shot or arrested. Mind if I sit?" he asked.

"How bout we fire up a small fire for some coffee. I'm kinda in a hurry but I guess we can talk for a while. My horse could use a rest anyway," Vince stated.

Vince rounded up some twigs and small branches and started a small fire.

"The town appointed a deputy until I can get there and get things sorted out," the Marshall stated. "There was plenty of citizens present when it all went down which cleared the man who was involved with all the shooting. It seems he's innocent on all counts."

"That's good to hear. My name is Vince by the way," Vince responded, again not revealing a last name.

"Matt," the Marshall introduced shaking Vince's hand.

The rest of the visit was mostly small talk. Vince told all about his father's ranch and his visit out West to be with a friend, leaving out all the details that could throw up a red flag. Two hours later the Marshall politely announced that he would have to leave to make a few more miles before making camp. He told Vince of a small town that could be reached before night fall.

The Marshall thanked Vince for the coffee and the time they passed.

"By the way, the man who cleaned up the town was riding a sharp paint with a fantastic tailored saddle," the Marshall stated as he spurred his horse.

Vince shook his head smiling watching the Marshall disappear down the trail. He realized how lucky he was.

The Marshall wasn't too far off on his estimated time to the next town. The trail was plenty rough though and Colt threw a shoe. That would have to be fixed as soon as they reached the next town.

Riding into town he noticed a man lighting the oil lamps which aligned the streets. The moon was only a quarter this night and not giving a whole lot of visibility. A light fog was rolling-in which meant the possibility of rain.

"Hi friend," Vince yell out. "Can you tell me what time the blacksmith will be in tomorrow?"

"Are you kidding," the man responded. "I am the blacksmith, but don't ask me for any favors until around eight tomorrow morning,"

"Deal. Is there a stall available for tonight?" Vince asked.

"Help your self," the smith responded.

"Name's Vince," Vince announced.

"Bonner," the smith returned.

Vince went about unsaddling Colt, wiped him down and then threw some fresh hay in the stall.

"See ya in the morning Bonner," Vince announced as he exited to find a hotel.

The streets were empty. Only piano notes filled the air.

Walking into the hotel, a man at the desk was already turning the guest book for Vince to sign.

"People play cards around here?" Vince asked.

"You shouldn't have a hard time finding a table to take your money," the clerk answered.

"You sound pretty positive I'll be leaving here broke," Vince remarked.

"Just made a comment, Mister Rodgers sir," the clerk answered as he read the name in the book.

Walking over to the saloon, he heard plenty of laughter from drinkers and women working their time. Entering, he noticed the bat doors were at the point of falling off the wore-out hinges. The squeal they gave out made sure no one could come in unnoticed. Slats were missing which Vince bet were removed by .45 caliber bullets which probably made for a bad night for some poor card player or drunk.

The place was nearly full. He quickly found a table with some who acted like regulars. A chair was kicked out and he was invited to sit-in. Vince saw the chair faced opposite the way he liked. He pulled a chair at the opposite side of the table and sat. All three men looked at him with curious expressions.

"Just get in?" one asked.

"About an hour ago," Vince answered.

The rest of the men took the hint and went back to playing cards. Vince played cautiously, being watchful of the cheaters as warned by the blacksmith. He was winning his share and a bit more. When he had a pile of bills in front of him he would fold some and slip them in his vest. He was winning about the same from each man and they seemed to be drinking more and not worrying about winning. The evening went by pretty fast. Talk was mostly between the three regulars.

The more everyone drank, the louder the drunks got. Bits and pieces from conversations from other tables alarmed Vince as he heard talk of three men. Not wanting to arise any suspicion, he tried to listen while pretending he was concentrating on what was going on at his table. He really didn't get much from the others but the mention of three guys had his attention. Glad he had taken his saddle to his room before coming to the saloon, he went on enjoying the card game.

He was two hundred ahead when he stood and excused himself for the evening.

Stretching with a slight yawn he wandered up to the bar for a last beer before turning in.

Two men were in a deep conversation and one was describing a gunfight at the next town east.

"Yeah, as I hear it two men rubbed shoulders at the bar the wrong way and next thing they were waiting for each to make the move. From what I hear, one was just a kid, both drew at the same time with both hitting their target and both dying right there at the bar. There were two others that hung back and watched. The sheriff gave them an hour to get out of town or be jailed as an accessory," the one man remarked.

"Know which way the other two went," Vince asked.

"East," the man responded while looking at Vince with some concern.

That was enough, he turned tail heading through the bat doors and out to the street.

Walking into the hotel he noticed the curious look he was getting from the clerk but decided to ignore it.

When he got to his room he very carefully checked the lock and anything else that would ensure his safety. Finding nothing, he went inside and locked the door behind him.

He slept like a log for a few hours. Half awake, he heard someone stop at his door. He could see the shadow of feet at the bottom of the door. Fully alert now, he pulled his pistol and laid there continuing to watch the door. The shadow of feet stayed for quite a while. Getting up, he dressed quickly, but by the time he got to open the door whoever was there had left.

Last night he was feeling good and relatively safe. So what and who was this? He thought through several possibilities but nothing made much sense. Was he safe or was this just a coincidence? Was there more to it that he didn't know about?

Before he went to breakfast he decided to visit the sheriff. Maybe he could make some sense of this.

Walking in, he found the sheriff sitting at his desk with a mug of coffee.

"Coffee?" the sheriff offered.

"Thanks don't mind if I do," Vince answered, walking over to the stove.

It was hot and black, just the way he liked it.

"Sit and take a load off your feet," the sheriff invited.

"Sheriff, I have a problem and thought I'd pass it by you to see what you think," Vince mentioned.

"There's not much that goes in town that isn't quickly spread around. It would be up to you to decide on its accuracy. Especially if you heard it last night when most men were drowned in alcohol," he proclaimed. "My names Fred, been the sheriff here for goin on almost three years."

"Vince, Vince Rodgers," Vince introduced himself.

"Go ahead Vince, what's on your mind?" the sheriff conceded.

Vince explained everything that happened since Albuquerque, feeling he didn't need to go back any farther.

"That's quite a story," Fred answered, scratching his head letting everything Vince said soak in. Well you're not too far off from the stories floating around. I did get a telegram about some trouble makers, warning me just in case they decided to double back to this area. I'm embarrassed to say, but that may have been my deputy at you door earlier. He spooks easy and isn't the bravest of men I know. If so, I hope you'll accept my apology."

Chapter 28

Jake had been mulling things over in his mind. He had hired three gunfighters to protect him. One had deserted him while another was shot and killed over a senseless bar fight. He was down to one man responsible for his safety which made it a one-on-one fight. This made Jake very uneasy. He had to come up with a plan, whether it was fair or not. To Jake even a back shot would work given the chance. Being victorious was more important than fairness. Not so when it came to a professional gunfighter with a reputation to protect. It would be face-to-face or nothing at all. Jake didn't have a back shooting gunfighter which gave him reason to worry. If this man failed, he would be alone and vulnerable. If only he wasn't involved with the murder of this man's family. He was quickly realizing that his partner wasn't going to stop until he was found and delt with. He was also in the dark since he didn't know it was Vince Masters that was coming fast and hard to meet up with him.

Desperate as a man could be, he offered half the money he made in cattle rustling if his pursuer would be taken care of. It was the deal of a life time to a lone gunfighter and was quickly accepted. Now all that was needed was to have the man with the fancy saddle come to him.

Still thinking scared, he felt like he needed to come up with alterative plans but keep them private just in case he got the chance to exercise them. No one would know. He was even having second thoughts of going home. Maybe head in another direction instead. He had plenty of money to keep him going. If he had any idea it was Vince Masters on his heels, his only choice would be to run. But he didn't. Instead his devious mind was exploring different ways to back shoot, or start a rock slide along one of the mountain passes. He would try anything that could stop this man before they met up. He didn't even have an idea which way he would be coming from, or when.

The constant worry was driving him crazy. He stayed extremely close to Bonner and needed to know where he was every minute. This was driving Bonner crazy to the point he had thoughts of killing Mike and taking all the money for himself. Being promised a big bonus when they got back to Arkansas, he thought better of it hoping it, was going to be worth his while. He had nowhere to go. Mike was not stingy with money so Bonner decided to follow the original plan and see it through.

If he only knew what was going through Mike's head. If Mike could find four more guns for hire, he definitely would and that for sure would be the last straw for Bonner. Mike knew this and would have to be very sneaky to try to pull that off behind Bonners back. He could find himself feeling the pain of a .45 boring its way through his chest. That would not be good. Bonner wasn't about to share money with anyone. The others were gone and he had brought Mike this far by himself.

Mike even thought of back shooting Bonner and then hire more men, but he was too much of a coward to try it. And he wasn't sure he could come up with more men. Bonner had the reputation and he would have to settle for that.

How long should he stay in Tulsa and wait for the man with the fancy saddle? He was beginning to panic and felt he needed high tail it home, or take to the north and hope his aggressor would give up the chase.

CHAPTER 29

The miles ticked-off as Vince headed east. He was heading straight to Tulsa. If lucky, he would arrive before Mike could figure what to do. He had at least two weeks of travel time. Not knowing where Mike was holding out, he decided Oklahoma City might be a place to stay for a week's rest.

The countryside was breathtaking and Vince was taking it all in, again wishing his family was there to enjoy it with him. He hurt inside when he witnessed things that he knew his family should be enjoying too. Colt sensed his sadness and gave a little buck to take Vince's mind off what ever was bothering him. Vince knew he had the best horse in the world. Who else had a horse whose owner and horse acted and re-acted in unison?

Watching Colt's head bob as he walked the trail, Vince knew Colt could care less how beautiful the weather was or how nice the scenery. The sound of Colt's hooves methodic clunking against the loose rocks on the trail was almost putting Vince in a trance. He was tiring early this day and decided to set camp for the night.

There was plenty of folage for Colt and privacy for a small fire. Vince formeda small a small teepee with branches and had it burning enough in minutes for the coffee pot sitting on a small flat rock. His meat was gone, so took out his rifle to see if he could scare up rabbit from the bushes. He hadn't gone fifty yards when his super bolted out almost straight in front of him he lifted the rifle and fired. He could now get a meal going with the few potatoes and biscuits remaining and fill his empty stomach before retiring. A half moon gave enough light to see shadows if anything or anyone came into their camp site.

Vince was asleep in minuets only to be suddenly awakened by a familiar noise he knew from many years on the trail. A hungry wolf smelled the food and felt the need to come into the camp and find it. Vince had his gun in his hand, watching Colt who was standing with ears at attention.

Vince didn't want to shoot a wolf just looking to survive. This was his turf after all. Bringing up his gun, he fired high over the wolf, scaring it off. Throwing a few larger branches on the fire he felt it safe enough now to sleep the rest of the night. Colt had jolted to the sound of shot but settled quickly. The sound of a nearby owl helped Vince relax and doze off for a deep sleep.

This night Vince had a dream that played-out with a warning. A stranger approached him with the intent to shoot it out. The man just laughed like he was going up against a tender foot kid just learning to shoot. The laugh got louder and louder. The man went for his gun. Vince saw flame expelling from the barrel as he leveled his gun and fanned a shot. No pain was felt as he stood there watching the man, still laughing. He was raising his gun for a second shot as Vince fanned three quick shots hitting his target each time. The man stood there laughing so loud now it woke Vince from his sleep. Glad to be awake, he laid there replaying the dream trying to make sense of it all. He was in no hurry to close his eyes. Laying there for quite some time he starred at the stars and let his mind wonder. Four shots and the man was still standing, laughing. This bothered Vince as he took this as a warning. He needed to travel with extra caution from here on out. Thinking hard, he tried to recognize the face of this dream assailant. If only he could remember some features of the man's face it might help him in the future. The only thing he could remember was the laugh. As far as the man's face, he kept drawing a blank. The man's clothing was a blur also. He tortured himself for quite awhile before falling back to sleep. The dark green sequence began again with Vince waking to a man pointing a gun in his face, firing point-blank. Bang! Sitting up in a full sweat he decided to walk around to help clear his mind of all this. When he came back to lay down, his mind was in another zone. He was thinking of his family and some of the pleasant things he experienced while they were still alive, again quietly falling back into a pleasant sleep. Next morning he woke refreshed, but still somewhat unsettled.

While making coffee he went back to thinking about the dream hoping he could remember something about the laughing gunman. He ate biscuits and drank his coffee in deep thought, glancing over to catch Colt looking at him as if he knew what was going through his mind. The day looked clear. As he broke camp he thought he saw the wolf in the near distance waiting for the camp to desert so he could come for any scraps left behind.

Leaving the camp site and getting back on the trail, he again gave Colt free reins, letting him walk at his own pace. This gave Vince time to look around, watch the mountains, and be alert for an ambush. It also gave him time to sort-out things in his mind and put things in perspective. Did his dreams have any real meaning? Would things happen in the near future or in the next month or two? He had to be on guard all the time as he was in for a long ride. Being a man who liked to go head to head with trouble he wasn't in a state of mind to deal with a coward.

After hours of open range riding he saw a lone man approaching him. Colt's head went erect and Vince went into a defensive mood. As they closed in on each other the man looked peaceful enough. Vince was a pretty good judge of character a bit of small talk would tell him if the rider was good or bad.

"Howdy partner," the man greeted as he approached.

"Morning to ya," Vince responded. "Been riding all night?"

"Heck no, camped quite a few miles back," the man returned. "Heading to Oklahoma City?"

"Yeah. Thought I'd stay a few days before heading on. I'm on my way out to Arkansas. How much farther is it to the city?" Vince asked inquisitively.

"Don't rightly know. A long way," the man responded teasing.

"Anything I should know of what's ahead?" Vince asked.

"No more than any other town," the man returned. "Good looking horse and that looks like quite an expensive saddle."

This observation put Vince on-guard. He glanced down at the man's gun high on his hip with a 45/40 settled in its sheath. This man was no gunfighter. This put Vince slightly at ease but he still kept his guard up.

"Thanks. I raised him from birth and he turned out to be quite a dependable pal," patting the side of Colt's neck thinking that was enough of a response.

"Won't take up any more of your time mister," the man excused himself. "It's just nice to see a friendly face from time to time."

"Stay safe," Vince offered.

Vince looked on ahead to see nothing but open range. He knew why the man said the city was a long way, but knew from experience time had its way of taking any trip mile by mile minute by minute, hour by hour.

Vince kept looking back at the man from time to time until he vanished over the horizon. He wondered where he was going, but knew it was none of his business. Why did he give a stranger so much information? Oh well, probably nothing to worry about. Hours went by but it seemed like he was going nowhere looking at what seemed to be the same scenery repeating itself. Looking for tree and bushes, he knew where to head for water. More than a few times he would take advantage of a few bigger pools by stripping down and jumping in to cool his body temperature down. The pools were sometimes very far apart so he took advantage whenever he could.

Two days more on the trail, feeling effects constant riding has on certain parts of his body he started wondering how much farther he had to go. Miles ahead he spotted a trail of dust coming toward him. This had to be a pack of riders or a stage coach to kick-up that much dust. It was a stage. As it got closer he got happier knowing he would soon know how much farther he had to go for the town. Finally it was a couple hundred feet in front of him. As he flagged the driver with his hat, he found a shotgun aimed at him as the driver drew back on the reins bringing the rig to a halt.

"What's the meaning of this?" asked the driver. "We're not supposed to stop for anyone."

"Sorry fellas," Vince conceded. "But I've been on the trail for a week now heading for Oklahoma City and would really like to know how much further it is? You'd be coming from there I'd guess."

"Keep riding at a steady pace and you should be there sometime tomorrow," the driver answered. "We got to get going mister, we're on a schedule. A warning to you also. Don't try to stop a stage out on the range, you could get shot."

"I can see that. It's just that my body is weary. I thought I'd have been there by now," Vince surrendered.

"Good day fella," the driver answered, snapping the reins, getting the team under way again.

Time on the trail went slowly and boring as the distance never seemed to change no matter how many mile he traveled. He found himself talking to Colt about nothing, in particular singing the same song over and over, not able to get the tune out of his head. He found himself whistling the same tune he had been singing. His head began hurting and aching to the point he wanted to dismount and walk for awhile. Sunset finally came and Vince couldn't get to a camp fast enough. His head was beating so bad he could hardly keep his eyes open.

He choose the first likely looking spot, tying extra lead, pulled the saddle and gave him a quick brush down. He proceeded to throw down his bed roll, flopped his throbbing head down and tried to sleep-off the weariness.

Feeling like minutes, it was actually hours later when he was awakened by hammering in the distance. Lying motionless for a few minutes, realizing his splitting headache had vanished he sat up. The hammering was definitely being made by a person. The quarter moon provided low level light that limited visibility. Quietly going through his saddle bags, he fished for his spy glass, then worked his way to a spot he could soon the area without being noticed.

He barely made out a silhouette of a man hammering a cross into the earth just off the trail. Continually watching, he saw the shadow go to his horse, get something resembling saddle bags or some kind of a pouch go back to shovel a hole and bury something. He then mounted his horse and continued west on the trail.

Vince laid low and stayed hidden the best he could hoping Colt didn't snort or make any kind of noise that might give them away. Colt stood still and quiet as the rider rode off. Vince waited for a good half hour, then wandered on foot over to the cross to check things out. The cross was hammered into the ground solidly, yet whatever was buried was kind of shallow as the man took only a short time digging. Getting down on his knees, he dug with his hands until he uncovered a set of saddlebags. Cautiously he opened the top bag and pulled out an oil wrapped piece of leather that was protecting a pile full of paper money which Vince thought was probably stolen. Wrapping-up the money, and tucking it back in the saddle bag, he proceeded to re-bury it. Seeing a rock near the cross, he pulled up the cross and walked it fifty paces west, parallel with the trail, then five paces to the left. He then hammered the cross back in a deep as the stranger did. Returning to where the bags were buried, he went across the path east 30 paces and kicked over a pile of cactus. When he went back to his makeshift camp he made a small map of what he just did and put it in his saddle bags. It was now time to break camp and continue on his way. He knew he didn't want to ride into a town with saddlebags of money without knowing what he was riding into. He would wait until he got into town, find out if the money had anything to do with the town, then maybe take the map and explain to the sheriff.

The weather clouded-over and it started to rain. Turning a bend in the trail, he saw he was just coming into the boundaries of town which put a full smile on Vince's face. Not even a soaking rain could dampen his spirit, knowing he could lay back for a few days, get a nice hot bath and enjoy some poker. "Let it rain as hard as it wants," Vince thought to himself as he first headed for the livery. The stable owner came to greet Vince and offered assistance which was instantly accepted.

"Where can I get a big great steak partner?" Vince asked as they were finishing with Colt.

"There's only one place for steak, The Shiny Nugget," the man responded without hesitation. "It's a good hotel too with nice rooms."

Vince threw the man a silver dollar and asked him to take care of his saddle, bridle. Grabbing his saddle bags, rifle and bed roll he headed to the recommended hotel. Walking into the dinning room, he gave his usual thorough scan, then found the table he felt to be safe. Checking each man one by one, evaluating each guilty he sat and ordered a steak; rare. He found that there were a few patrons checking him out as well, but being new in town that would be expected. His steak dinner came and he found the stable owner knew what he was talking about. It was a long, dirty, uncomfortable ride but it was all forgot after such a great meal. Washing it down with three cups of coffee, he sat and watched giving his body some time to digest what he just ate before heading to the gambling tables for some relaxing poker.

The saloon was well lit. Walking through the bat wings he knew there was some serious card players at the tables. Three bored saloon gals surrounded him before he reached the bar.

After a quick look around the room, he sensed the need to keep his guard up. No special reason, but the dream of the night before stayed with him every minute. He tried hard to recall the face or even the clothes the man wore in his dream to give him a chance to prepare himself. Ordering a beer, he anxiously waited, then drank it down like it was water and quickly ordered another.

The long trail ride wore him down. It was time to allow his body to rest to get his muscles back in shape.

He found a table with an empty seat near the back of the room. Walking over, he asked if he could join in for a few hands and was quickly accepted. There was quite a bit of money laid all around the table so he figured the stakes were high. Probably a game where there was no limit. Was this standard poker in a big town? He laid a stack of bills in front of him as the deck was placed in front of him. He just happened to sit at this game as the deck passed to him for shuffling and dealing.

"Five card stud?" he asked.

"Been playing it most of the night," a thin wrinkled man called Jim answered.

Vince shuffled, then laid the deck down to have the man next to him cut the deck. He then combined the two stacks and commenced dealing. He was being watched closely by a couple of the players, just as he would be when they delt. The deck went around the table a couple of times before all of them won each others trust. Thry then all relaxed to enjoy the game. In minutes he figured out most of the men at the table were regulars and played here often. If any one knew of a robbery in this town, it would be these three. He tried not to start conversation too quickly, but instead paid close attention to the conversation around the table. It wasn't long before he started to hear bits of interest, but it wasn't about robbery or stolen money. It was about a gunfighter looking for a stranger coming east from Colorado. No names were mentioned. It was just a story that was spreading around town.

"Anybody know the gunfighter's name?" Vince asked with enthusiasm

"Bonner. That's his name," one of the players answered.

"It's rumored Bonner is waiting for his target in Tulsa. Others say he's right here in town, yet no one has seen him in this area," another retorted.

"So there's someone around that knows what this Bonner guy looks like?" Vince asked.

"Poster in the Sheriff's office is an actual picture, not a sketch, if that would interest you," the same man responded.

Vince figured he'd go visit the sheriff's office in the morning. Maybe the sheriff would mention something about a recent robbery. He didn't know what his next move was if he couldn't get a lead on the money he found.

Tulsa would be as good as any place to meet up with this Bonner and Jake. It was the last stretch of his trip before returning to his father's ranch. He thought he should send a telegraph, announcing his return giving warning. Thinking that could be dangerous, he decided against it.

Walking down to the Sheriff's office he noticed what a nice town this was. He would have liked to hang out and play some poker with the guy's.

At the sheriff's office door he was met by a big old yellow dog. The dog had knotty hair with bare spots over portions of his body. He looked like a deserted street dog. Looking up at Vince with sad eyes, "Give me some food," he seemed to be saying. Vince figured he'd get some scraps from the dinner if he was still hanging around after he left the sheriff. As he walked by the dog gave a low but warning growl. Vince gave a half smile and mimicked a growl back.

Vince walked back to the door and slammed it shut.

"What in tar nation?" the sheriff yelled jumping to his feet.

"My name is Vince, Vince Rodgers," he announced using his alias.

"What can I do for ya?" the sheriff asked.

"I was told you may be able to help me with a problem," Vince responded. "I'm being hunted by a man by the name of Bonner. I don't know what he looks like and was told you have a wanted poster of him."

"And why would it be he's hunting you and not you him?" the sheriff asked inquisitively.

"Well he's traveling with a man responsible for my wife's and son's death. This man hired four gunfighters for his personal protection. This Bonner is the last of the three. I heard he's hold-up in Tulsa but might be here instead. I wouldn't know," Vince conceded.

"And the other three?" the sheriff asked.

"Dead," Vince answered.

"Legally I hope," the sheriff returned.

"Of course, I gave them the chance to draw first. It wasn't on account of the reward because I never collected a cent. I just wanted to stay alive," Vince answered.

"I guess I can believe you. I don't think you'd be here otherwise," the sheriff responded.

"Well, do you have a poster on this Bonner? I'd sure like it to know who's gunning for me," Vince conceded.

The sheriff shuffled some papers on his desk and hesitated glancing at it for bit before handing it over to Vince.

"This is Bonner," he said as Vince took it from his hand.

The men at the bar were right. The photo was clear and Vince would not forget the face starring back at them.

Handing it back the sheriff declined it.

"Keep it. I don't think I'll be needing it. I hope he is in Tulsa. I don't need any gun play in this town," the sheriff said.

Vince folded it and tucked it into his vest pocket.

"Well, if he's not in town, I'll be leaving in the morning for Tulsa," Vince informed. "I don't want him to leave before I get there. I'm tired of this and need to get it over with."

"If you, I'll telegraph on ahead and see what I can find out," the sheriff offered.

"Not unless you can do it quietly," Vince pleaded.

"Of course," the sheriff responded.

"Thanks for your help Sheriff. You probably won't see me again. I'll be on my way to Tulsa by daylight," Vince said.

"If I get a telegraph before you leave, I'll be sure to get it to you," the sheriff said.

"Thanks again," Vince said as he turned heel and went for the door.

Stopping short, he felt this was a good time to ask about the money he found.

"Sheriff, have you had any hold-up, bank or stage coach robbing lately," he asked.

"As a matter of fact I got a telegraph from Mustegee," the sheriff responded. "There was a stage carrying a payroll box hit just out of town. No one was killed but the payroll box was taken."

"Why do you ask?" the sheriff inquired.

Vince handed the map to him and told him about what he saw and what he did. If he sent a pose out to observe the area, for sure they would get the money first, then the men who stole it.

Exiting to the street he was met by a growl from the same old yellow dog.

"I'll be back in a bit," Vince said to the dog patting him on his head as he passed, not at all intimidated.

Back at the restaurant, he searched for and found the cook. Explaining what he needed, the cook was happy to oblige. Assuring him it wasn't a normal request. When Vince returned to the sheriff's office he found the dog waiting as if expecting him. Vince gave him the scraps a little at a time so the dog could enjoy the meal knowing it would be awhile before receiving another as good.

Morning came quickly and Vince was on the trail for Tulsa.

CHAPTER 30

Vince figured a little over three days to get to Tulsa. He thought back to when he had a partner with him on his travels. Jeb was his best friend, but was now settled in life as a rancher. Jane, his late wife was his trail companion and also his best friend. Robert, his son, he would pass all his knowledge onto as he grew from a boy to a man. Yet, now, here he was alone on the trail. Not totally alone. Riding the next best thing to a best friend was his horse. He raised Colt from birth, so he was part of him; his best friend and traveling partner. Those thoughts kept him occupied enough to keep his mind focused, enough to help make the days fly by. Sleeping was a problem, so he would ride until he was ready to drop. This assured him a good night's sleep.

Riding into sight of the town of Tulsa Vince thought to him self that he was only a six day ride to his dads' ranch. His ranch. There was only one thing between him and home. He was more than ready to eliminate that problem as soon as possible. Riding down Main Street he gave Colt free reins while he cautiously checked all the windows, doorways, alley's, anything that could hide an ambusher.

The town seemed quiet but Vince knew if the men he was looking for were here it was going to get quite busy real soon. If the men moved-on he would again have to, track them and wait for another time. He made sure he could be seen with Colt sporting the saddle his assailants would be looking for. This bothered Vince little because he knew what both the men looked like. His adrenalin was at high scale and he had high confidence of his abilities. He hoped to find the two men in the saloon. Inside he knew the job at hand wouldn't be easy. No gunfighter that lived to old age could afford to make mistakes.

No, Vince knew he was in for a fight and if he wanted survive, he would have to stay on his guard as much as Bonner, the gunfighter or Jake, the coward would be.

Tying Colt in front of the saloon he chanced that Colt and his saddle would be recognized. He walked in and up to the bar, ordering a beer. The bartender gave him a suspicious look but he didn't challenge it. He was thirsty and as he downed the first beer he was only thinking of how good it tasted. Sliding the empty mug to the center of the bar the bartender quickly poured him another. Vince would hold at two beers in order to stay sharp. Just in case.

He heard the batwings swing open. The two men walked reflecting the big mirror behind the bar. He knew the taller one was Jake Ballard, which would make the other man, Bonner. Not thinking he would be shot in the back, he slowly finished his beer. Setting it down, he slowly turned to face his adversaries.

"Well, we finally meet up," Vince announced.

"Yeah. You killed my brother. What did you think? You'd just ride off into the sunset and live the good life?" Jake bellowed.

"Nope. I've been looking for this day more than you. You're responsible for killing my wife and son. Now you'll pay," Vince retorted.

You could have heard a pin drop as the patrons all stood in silence after hearing what Vince said. These two killed an innocent woman and her child?

Jake and Bonner saw the reaction of everyone that just heard what was said. Jake panicked thinking he and Bonner were in big trouble. He was right.

No one said a thing as Jake stepped back and expected Bonner, the gunfighter, to them through this situation.

Bonner stood fast, slipping the strap from the hammer of his pistol, standing with his feet spread slightly. He was now in fighting stance and confident of his ability to survive.

Vince was done talking. He had already removed the loop from his pistol hammer before entering the bar. He was ready and watched for any twitch or movement from Bonner.

The two stood fast, anticipating each others move. What seemed like minutes were only seconds. Jake was sliding his feet back toward the exit in hopes no one would notice. He was successful as he turned and bolted like the coward he was.

Bonner paid him no mind as he concentrated on Vince. It was totally his business now. Doing what he got paid for. Survive another gunfight and move on. In the back of his mind however, he was thinking he would still be in trouble now no matter the out come of this fight. He was exposed as a cold blooded killer. A crime he was not responsible for, but no one around him in the saloon knew that.

Not thinking, he went for his gun, at the same instant realizing a fatal mistake. Lacking full concentration, the speed of which his gun could be pulled would be a bit slower and would end his life.

If he knew Vince Masters ability, he would have known he didn't have a chance no matter what state of mind he was in.

The blast of Vince's gun filled the saloon with an ear shattering explosion. He fanned it a second time with so much vengeance; he didn't realize what he was doing. When the third shot kicked his pistol back, his mind caught up to his actions. He stood there with a smoking gun, watching his target fall to the floor, never getting his gun to shooting status.

The patrons could only grasp their ears, waiting for the ringing to stop.

Vince hadn't realized Jake had slipped out the door and disappeared.

What everyone witnessed was so memorable. There had been gunfights in this town many times. Johnny Ringo was one of the most famous gunfighters believed to have been in a shoot-out on the streets of Tulsa. But the speed of Vince Masters was such that it would be talked about for years.

It took a few moments before Vince collected his composure, slipping his pistol back into its holster.

Quickly, the saloon was buzzing with everyone talking of what they just experienced. The story constantly changed, describing Vince's fast draw. Within minutes, it was almost as if Vince's draw was a magic trick.

When the sheriff arrived, one thing was for sure; everyone saw Bonner draw first.

As for Jake, he was gone and Vince knew there was no use looking for him. A coward like that could hide in a rat hole knowing the trouble he was in. He didn't think Jake was brave enough to go to the stable to get his horse or even be in the state of mind to steal one. Jake was going nowhere, at least not on this day. Turning to the bar, he saw he had a beer waiting for him knowing he wouldn't have to buy another as long as he stayed in town. It was safe now so he had two or three more while explaining to the sheriff his version of what happened. Vince was constantly interrupted by men coming up and trying to buy him a drink. To become a friend with the fasted gun they ever witnessed. This was the man they would say they knew personally as they exaggerated the stories.

That night Vince laid in bed thinking way back of the time when he and his brother Cal were in the fight with the Ballards. The sheriff took care of the out-come of that fight. This one would be finished by him self. He was looking forward to.

Suddenly, he had a mindful warning. What if Jake hired other guns to assassinate him? Why didn't the think of that before? He had put himself in a vulnerable spot earlier and didn't realize it. Lucky thing the sheriff showed up so fast, he could have been cut- down. Not been able to defend him self. Stupid! Real stupid! Well, he got away with it, this time, but he wouldn't let his guard down like that ever again.

His thoughts went back to Jake and the idea of where he could have gone off to hide. He was real tired, but couldn't fall asleep no matter how much he tried. He had a knotted stomach, not knowing what to do, where to look, or who he might have to watch- out for. The town was upset about the information they overheard at the gunfight. Word was spreading fast, this may detour Jake. Or another hired gun from proceeding with another attempt on Vince's life.

Whether he slept or not, he decided to get up early, get some breakfast and begin his search for Jake.

Early morning found Vince heading over to the diner. He was greeted by many patrons already seated. They had compassion for Vince and wanted to help him anyway they could. If he only realized how much they wanted to solve his problem for him, he could have gone back to his fathers' ranch and left the problem to the town people. But that wasn't Vince's style.

Leaving the diner Vince, walked-out to the street. The sun was bright, promising to be a beautiful day. Vince walked over to the sheriff's office to check on any news. Walking-in there was a cup of coffee waiting for him.

"Saw you coming from across the street. Figured you may have room for another cup," the sheriff announced.

Before Vince got a sip of coffee a young man came scurrying into the office.

"Sheriff. We had one of our best horses stolen last night. Pretty sure it was that man with the gunfighter this fellow shot," he reported.

"Damn,' Vince said with much disgust. I knew he would get out of here one way or another. He's just that lucky," Vince responded.

"Not so lucky. The horse belongs to my brother and that fella made a big mistake stealing his horse," the man said. "He won't get far, I'll tell ya that much."

"I don't want anybody taking the law into their own hands," the sheriff warned.

"There is no law for a horse thief. Surely if the man did what Vince here said he did, he should be hanging from the first tree available," he retorted.

"I'll get that verified and the men responsible will be held accountable," the sheriff warned.

Listening to all this, Vince wanted to hit the trail and find this man before the others. Nothing would please him more than to break his neck, and bring justice to a coward and peace to his mind. To know Jane and Richard could now rest in peace.

He and his friends wouldn't. They would make sure that it looked like self defense just like the shooting last night. They'll try to bring him back to face a hanging offense for horse stealing, but if he resists, he'll be coming back tied across the saddle.

Vince knew he had to get going if he wanted to get Jake before the man's brother did. He thought the sheriff was thinking the same thing but knew it was going to be hopeless. These men were not to be messed with and legally he couldn't do anything, but he knew what to expect. Not blaming them, but he decided he best get out and look for this Jake fella and hope he could find him first.

Chapter 31

Jake was riding the horse to a quick death. He knew he was in a lot of trouble. Known by many now, his reputation was fully exposed by Vince. There was no place for him to go. No where would he be safe. It would be nearly impossible to hire a gunslinger for protection with the warrants the states had out for him.

Worst of all, he didn't get to grab anything he owned when he fled town. That included all the stashed money. He was totally broke in money as well as spirit. He couldn't go home. The embarrassment would be unbearable. He was scarred. Wondering to him self if there was a place he could go. A place to be safe!

Mexico was his only choice now and it was the one place he didn't want to go. There would be men covering the border. Even if he made it into Mexico he knew he would be assassinated. This man or someone would not stop searching for him until he was hanging from a tree. He wouldn't even make it to a court of law.

The horse he stole was beginning to foam at the mouth. Soon Jake would be walking. Pulling back on the reins he brought the horse to a halt. The horse fell as he dismounted and Jake knew he wouldn't be getting up. Taking his pistol he aimed and fired. The blast was loud. Echoing between the mountain range, it would be heard a long way. Another mistake made by not thinking clear.

Sitting next to the dead horse he sat and came near to tears. He heard the sound of a lone horse. He wouldn't be going much farther now. They had come for him. He looked up to see a lone horseman riding straight to him, still some distance away.

He couldn't get himself to pick up the gun to defend himself. He sat there watching the rider getting closer.

Vince could see Jake now. He saw the condition he was in.

"Go ahead. Shoot!" Jake yelled, half crying

"That would be too good for you Jake," Vince answered. "I'm gonna beat you to death with my bare hands."

Vince dismounted and unbuckled his gun belt, laying it over his saddle.

All of a sudden desperation overcame Jake. He knew he couldn't out-shoot this man, but he knew he had a chance in a fist fight. He had been fighting with his hands his whole life and many fights.

"You don't recognize me, do you Jake Ballard?" Vince asked.

Jake looked but nothing was registering.

"No. Should I?" Jake asked. "Why should I know you?"

"My name is Vince Masters," Vince announced.

Jake felt like he was kicked in the stomach. He began to recognize the man. Not clearly, but enough to realize he was in the toughest spot in his life.

Jake started to recover a bit. He knew he couldn't out-shoot this man, but from what he remembered, he beat his brother years ago and he felt good about his chances of beating this man. Standing, he began to gather his composure. He was feeling embarrassed to have let this man see him cowering. In a few minutes it wouldn't matter. He would beat this man to death with his fists. He wouldn't be telling anyone anything. Walking up to Vince throw a punch that if connected would have ended it, here and now.

Vince side stepped the punch and retaliated with one of his own, hitting his mark with the same accuracy he could with his gun. Jake staggered back but to Vince's surprise, didn't go down. Jake stepped forward with a responding punch that knocked Vince back a few steps. Feeling as if he was just kicked by a mule, he thought he better quickly hit back with a lot more power.

This was the man who responsible for Jane's and Roberts' death. When his next punch landed it was with all the power he had. Again Jake staggered back but not down. Jake came forward and Vince nailed him again, square on his chin. This time Jakes' body left the ground, landing on both feet bringing a round house of his own to Vince's face. Vince didn't know what held him up. This man hit harder than expected. Maybe he should have just shot him. Jake came hard and strong again. Vince was ready and straight armed a punch straight to the stone carved face. The man would was giving him a real fight. Jake fell back and crashed into Colt. Colt bucked making Jake lose his balance, knocking him to the ground. Jake shook the cobwebs from his head and saw Vince's gun fall from Colts' saddle, right next to him. He wasted no time grabbing the gun from the holster. Vince couldn't believe his eyes. How could this have happened? He could now only wait for the blast and die. Everything suddenly went wrong. The blast was ear shattering, the fight was over.

Vince froze waiting for the pain, the blood, death. There was none. He looked to see Jake in a sitting position with a red spot, growing, covering his chest.

Bewildered, he stood there and watched.

"You can thank me later," he heard off to his back.

He turned to see three men sitting on their horses. Apparently they had ridden up during the fight unnoticed and decided to watch. That is until the man decided to cheat and use a gun to win a fist fight.

"Teach him to steal my horse," the man said, all looking at each other. "My name is Johnny Sauters. That's my horse there. I just saved him from a hanging. Help save your life from such a coward also," he stated.

It was over Vince thought. His face was too sore to think of much else.

"He's your kill," Vince announced. "You may as well take him back with you. There should be quite a reward on him. It's yours."

Vince watched as the three lifted the body up over the saddle and tied him fast. When they were out of sight, he mounted Colt and headed home, back to the family ranch in Pinewood, Arkansas.

He made no announcement he was coming home. Riding through the ranch entrance gate, he saw that nothing much had changed. Off to the left he saw a couple of riders tying their horses in front of the bunk house.

The front door of the main house opened and Ben walked out. At first he didn't believe his eyes. He was at Vince's side as he dismounted Colt. He grabbed Vince's hand for a shake and pulled him in for a big hug at the same time.

"Damn boy, I was wondering if I'd ever see you again. You look good, bigger than when you left. How do you explain that?" Ben asked.

"I still eat good, but I'm one tired hombre," Vince responded. "It's good to be home. Looks just like the same place I left three years ago.

"Three years. Boy how time flies," Ben exclaimed. "Come on in, we've got a lot of catchin-up to do."

Vince let Ben do most of the talking and listened to how Ben had built the ranch to an additional fifteen hundred head of prime cattle. Here, the best breed of quarter horses in the area. He explained that the men were out delivering twenty five hundred head to Amarillo, Texas.

Ben excused himself saying he needed to run up to the bunk house and would be right back.

Vince made his way to his Dad's office and made him self comfortable in the big cushy chair behind the big cherry desk. He sat there starring at the picture of his dad and of Katie with her horses, none of which had been taken down. Nothing was touched. Everything was just the way he left.

Sitting there, he knew Cal should be the one sitting in this chair. He knew he didn't fit this life style. Not now, not three years ago.

He waited until Ben returned and excused himself saying he needed to head up-stairs and get some sleep.

"Go ahead Vince. We'll talk more tomorrow," Ben ordered.

"Within minutes, staring at the ceiling, Vince knew he didn't belong. As soon as he could get things straight with Ben and his lawyer Mr. Bronson, he knew he would be leaving. Where? He didn't know, but he knew he needed to get away.

Jamie, he thought. Maybe that's where he was destined to go.